The Torment of Billy Tate

The Rogue Exorcist

Book Two

Rick Wood

Blood Splatter Press

Also By Rick Wood

The Sensitives
The Sensitives
My Exorcism Killed Me
Close to Death
Demon's Daughter
Questions for the Devil
Repent
The Resurgence
Until the End

The Rogue Exorcist
The Haunting of Evie Meyers
The Torment of Billy Tate
The Corruption of Carly Michaels

Blood Splatter Books
Psycho B*tches
Shutter House
This Book is Full of Bodies
Home Invasion
Haunted House
Woman Scorned
This Book is Full of More Bodies
He Eats Children

Cia Rose
When the World Has Ended
When the End Has Begun
When the Living Have Lost
When the Dead Have Decayed

The Edward King Series
I Have the Sight
Descendant of Hell
An Exorcist Possessed
Blood of Hope
The World Ends Tonight

Anthologies
Twelve Days of Christmas Horror
Twelve Days of Christmas Horror Volume 2
Roses Are Red So Is Your Blood

Standalones
When Liberty Dies
The Death Club

Sean Mallon
The Art of Murder
Redemption of the Hopeless

Chronicles of the Infected
Zombie Attack
Zombie Defence
Zombie World

Non-Fiction
How to Write an Awesome Novel
The Writer's Room
Horror, Demons and Philosophy

© Copyright Rick Wood 2023

Cover design by bloodsplatterpress.com

With thanks to my Advance Reader Team

No part of this book may be reproduced without express permission from the author

MANY YEARS AGO

Prologue

Everyone is celebrating.

Everyone who knows what's happened, that is.

A giant wave of relief has cast itself over all those who are aware.

The biggest threat to humanity is gone. The world is safe. The mass population, completely unaware of the threat, can continue to live their lives in blissful ignorance of the forces that fight in the darkness. They can avert their eyes from the shadows, never having to look too hard at what lurks behind them.

The Edward King War is over.

The attempt of The Devil to unleash his antichrist into the world had failed. The man he'd conceived to be the Heir of Hell, to bring Armageddon to the human population, to allow demons into the human realm so they can devour every soul—it was done. Hell had lost. And everyone was glad.

Everyone, that was, except Father Thomas Hanley.

Hanley had forced his smiles, shook all the hands, congratulated those involved—he'd done his duty of thanking God, leading everyone in prayer, and rejoicing in their victory.

Except, he didn't feel he had much to rejoice about.

There was a niggling doubt preventing him from celebrating with the same enthusiasm as everyone else.

It was a feeling—the kind of feeling that simmers in your gut and rises through your stomach, leaving an uneasy sickness that lingers and boils—that this was not over.

Surely, they couldn't all believe The Devil would leave it there.

Surely, they couldn't believe The Devil would fail to leave an insurance plan.

As the night faded to morning, Hanley remained in his chair, at his desk, in the darkness of his study, his chin resting on his hand, his pensive expression focussed on the corner of the room—not that there was anything in that corner; he could have been focussing on any aspect of the room, and he would not see it. His mind was too distracted to acknowledge the bin, or the wallpaper, or the book left open in front of him. His thoughts were somewhere else.

It couldn't be this simple.

He knows what they'd say—that it hadn't been simple. That they'd had to go to war with the antichrist, and they had lost good people, and they had come close to failing.

But they had succeeded. Against The Devil. The most powerful epitome of evil that exists. Against a plan he'd been working on for two thousand years.

How is that possible?

They were mortals. Against what was, essentially, a demonic god. And they'd won.

It just seems so... improbable... and no matter how much he recounts events, the ending makes little sense to him.

With a sigh, an exhalation of exasperation, he stands, draws apart the curtains, and watches as the thick black of night gives way to the first sign of dawn. He feels chilly, like one often does so early in the morning.

He goes over it again in his mind. Over everything. The battle by the swing set; the army fighting the demons; the presence of Balam. It wasn't easy, but it still wasn't hard enough.

He steps away from the desk, scans the book shelf, finds the nearest Bible, and opens it.

He knows every reference to the antichrist there is, such was the thoroughness of his research, and he checks each one individually for signs that his unease was justified.

1 John 4:3, This is the spirit of the antichrist, which you heard was coming and now is in the world already.

Revelation 13:5, And the beast was given a mouth uttering haughty and blasphemous words, and it was allowed authority for forty-two months.

Daniel 11:37, He shall pay no attention to any other god, for he shall magnify himself above it all.

All passages he has already read, studied, and scrutinised. It was his role in this war to understand the scripture's teaching of the antichrist; to acknowledge what it says, and to convey the wisdom he gleaned from it to those who needed to know.

But it feels like there's something he hasn't acknowledged. Something he hasn't conveyed. Something he has not told those who need to know.

And, in a moment of grave brilliance, the exact passage he requires comes to him, and leaves him struck with its clarity.

He turns to 2 Thessalonians 2:9, and he reads:

The coming of the lawless one is by the activity of Satan with all power and false signs and wonders, and with all wicked deception for those who are perishing, because they refused to love the truth and so be saved.

He highlights the keywords in this passage: false signs; wonders; wicked deception for those who are perishing.

Many had perished. There were casualties. And there were many false signs.

And he realises, in this moment, exactly what the wicked deception is.

"Edward King was not the only one..."

There is another.

He leaps to his feet. Runs to the banister, collects his hat and coat, ties his shoelaces in a hurry, and rushes to the front door. He swings it open, ready to start his car and rush to the Church, hurry to make sure people know there was more to come. Although the threat is not imminent, and may not present itself for decades, they need to know now; for this is the moment they can still prevent it; this is when they can find the *other* and vanquish the threat.

But he cannot leave the house.

For when he opens the door, his exit is blocked.

It's something between a wolf and a rabid dog. Its body hunches over. Saliva drips from its bared teeth. It growls, and its eyes lock with his.

"For without dogs, and sorcerers, and whoremongers, and murderers, and idolaters, and whoever loveth and maketh a lie..."

The quote from Revelations passes his lips, not in a statement of fight, but in an understanding of why this ravenous dog stands on his porch.

And he understands, as he looks into the beast's eyes, that this is the end. That the knowledge he has will die with him, and that no one will know.

This isn't acceptance, it's simply the burden of knowledge.

He closes his eyes.

And the beast pounces.

It rips skin from his muscle, muscle from his bone, and limbs from his body—and it continues to do so long after his last breath.

The Devil's creature ensures there is nothing left of the man.

His neighbours find him later, his chewed face lying across the doorway rudely distracting them from their daily routine. The newspapers report of a freak accident, a mauling by a wild dog—despite no wild dogs ever having been reported in the area.

His parishioners mourn the loss.

And no one knows.

At least, not yet.

Until, one day, what Hanley learned comes to fruition—and the world learns that it still has a debt to pay.

SIX MONTHS AGO

One

Thousands of pieces of sleet bombard the family home, colliding with windows, streaking across the street, fired like bullets cutting through a silent night.

Inside the house, silence is the enemy.

Inside the house, silence is all they have.

Inside the house, every creak and every moan of the floorboard and every deep croak of breath is an ominous warning of an assailant coming closer.

Jennifer buries herself in the corner of the cupboard, her fingers wrapped around her child's arms, pulling the toddler's body closer to hers.

The child cries—at least, she wants to—but Jennifer insists on silence.

Silence is crucial.

Her child buries her face in her mother's dress. The silk grows wet from her soundless sobs, and Jennifer strokes the child's hair.

She knows what's going to happen.

She is at a dead end. The corner of a cupboard. There is nowhere else she can hide.

He will find them.

It is inevitable.

He's changed so quickly, and he doesn't even seem to be aware of it. Years as a wonderful father and a doting husband, replaced by a week of cowering in corners. She was becoming used to hiding them both in the smallest space, weeping without noise, holding each other tight, desperate not to be found.

He was a kind man who would protect his family to the ends of the earth.

She has no idea what has caused this change in him.

"Jennifer..."

She can't locate the voice. It's not in the bedroom, that much is certain, but beyond that, she does not know. She imagines him walking across the hallway, slowly, teasing her, teasing himself, cackling, grinning, knowing the power he has, getting high off it, getting aroused by it.

Why does he have to do this?

She loves him. She always has. She's been a faithful, loving wife. Her friends adore him. Her family thinks he's wonderful. She's done everything she can to make him happy.

Yet this side of him still appeared, so suddenly, a few days ago, like a sudden illness. How can a good man change so quickly, and so drastically?

"Mummy, I'm scared..."

She holds her daughter close and begs her not to make a sound.

She wants to say it's going to be okay, that she will be fine, that there's nothing to worry about.

But she also doesn't want to lie.

So she rests her child's head against her chest, stroking her blond hair, closing her eyes and dropping her head back and wondering how they got to this point.

Surely he's going to realise, at some point, what he is doing.

He's going to, she knows it.

And then he'll stop and beg for forgiveness.

"*Tilly...*"

Her daughter flinches at the sound of her name.

When a father says his daughter's name, it should be a moment of comfort, a welcoming to his arms; it should elicit a feeling of happiness.

It elicits nothing but dread.

A feeling that the worst is yet to happen.

She hates herself for the trauma her child has experienced. For what she has had to witness, for what she has had to endure. But, mostly, she hates herself for letting it get to this point.

A door slams open. Not the bedroom, but one further down the hallway. The bathroom, maybe. A boot into the wood and the impact against the wall makes her jump, makes Tilly jump, and she feels her child quivering, shaking in her arms, and she holds her closer.

But it doesn't stop the child from shaking.

Because she knows her mother can't protect her. That, no matter how much her mother holds her close, her father will still have his way. That there will be no reprieve. That her mother's arms are pointless; a meaningless gesture; an empty comfort.

She knows her mother will not save her, and the thought fills her mother with anguish.

Another kick, another slam, and this time it's the bedroom next to hers. Tilly's bedroom. The cot in the centre, a mobile above it, colourfully painted walls he'd made sure were ready for the moment they arrived with their new baby. He'd put the cot together and the new cupboard and the mobile—everything was created by his hand, lovingly crafted for the enjoyment of their child.

She hears the cot smash. Imagines him upturning it. Ruining the creation he put together with such passion, such love.

And she hears the creaks of the floorboards.

This bedroom is next.

Tilly's shaking becomes increasingly vigorous.

She goes to tell her daughter not to worry, then realises they are empty words.

Why shouldn't her daughter worry?

Jennifer is worrying, after all.

The bedroom door slams open. It's louder than she remembers it.

A little light seeps through the crack between the doors of the cupboard.

"Jennifer... Tilly..."

He knows.

He knows where they are.

He knows they are terrified.

The cupboard door swings open. Tilly cries out. Jennifer stares. Light from the streetlamp outside the window forces him into a silhouette. He towers over them, darkness covering his grin.

He has a knife in his hand. A large butcher's knife.

Why does he have a knife?

"Please..."

He reaches for Jennifer, and she braces herself, her body tensing. But he doesn't take her. He takes the child instead.

"No! Please, no!"

She reaches out for Tilly.

He points his knife at the centre of her chest and Jennifer halts, on her knees, halfway to retrieving her daughter.

Tilly cries and begs and pleads.

Can he not hear her? Can he not see what he is doing?

"Billy, please..."

He puts the knife beside their daughter's throat.

"Billy, no! Don't!"

His grin widens. Becomes more lecherous. More sinister.

"Billy, you don't want to hurt our daughter..."

But he does. And he tries. Raises the knife in the air, aims it at Tilly's neck.

Jennifer dives toward her child, desperate to save her, the first time she's ever shown such bravery in the face of such wrath, and she grabs her child, holds her close, ensures that her body remains between the knife and her daughter, and she takes Tilly to the floor.

And a painful sensation pierces her back.

She feels warmth.

She realises it's blood trickling down her dress, making it thick. It sticks to her skin. The pain intensifies.

Her husband screams and another searing pain shoots into her back. And another. And another.

She collapses.

Tries to get back up, but she can't.

"Mummy..."

The voice is distant.

A flash of light and the pain is now in the side of her neck, and she's choking.

She can't breathe.

She stares at Tilly. Holds her child's eyes until the end.

Tries to beg him not to hurt her.

But she can't speak. She can't muster words. A mouthful of blood stops anything else from dribbling out of her mouth.

It fades to black, but she fights it. Refuses to accept it.

But it will happen, whether or not she fights it.

And the last thing she sees—the very last sight her mind registers—is the image of her husband—Tilly's hair in his fist

—Tilly's look of fear—and the knife in his other fist—falling toward her child.

Then there is no more fight, and emptiness is all she knows.

Her last thoughts are of her husband and her daughter, and how much he swore he loved them, how much he said he'd protect them, how much he promised to keep them safe.

Then it's over.

And she's just another statistic.

NOW

Two

I sit alone in the lecture theatre.

There are many people around me, but there are several empty seats between me and them. I don't blame them. I am clearly not one of them.

They are academics. Educated and well-dressed. Even those wearing jeans and a shirt look like they have ironed their jeans to excess, and their shirts are neat and well-fitted. I sit here, in my old, tatty jeans that have never seen an iron, my creased white t-shirt, and my leather biker jacket. I look like a person they would turn away from as we crossed in the street.

And they are young. All of them. University students or aspiring scholars. I am in my mid-thirties, though I imagine I look older. My tatty beard, my marked skin and my scruffy hair show exactly what a few years of fighting demons does to you.

At the front, Dr Olivia Chase delivers a lecture on demonology—a woman similar to my age, though she looks better for it, who wears a black pin-stripe power suit designed to show everyone that she is not easily intimidated. I thought it would be interesting to attend a talk on demonology; I thought it might extend some useful academic insights into the world I inhabit, and help inform the misinformed. Yet almost everything she has said has an element of untruth about it. Her lecture has been riddled with errors, and either she is a charlatan, or she does not know enough about the subject she claims to have a PhD in.

(Which is Theology. Her research is apparently focused on the identification and eradication of demons in medieval Britain compared to modern day—something that should have really given her far better knowledge than she is showing.)

She clicks her wireless presentation clicker, and her PowerPoint displays the next slide. Each image has the same border taken from the same PowerPoint template, and it makes her presentation look like it was designed by a child. The image itself is of a young woman, possibly mid-teens, lying on a bed. She has bags under her eyes and reaches her hand toward the sky.

"This was Karen Kayliss, a fourteen-year-old girl from Middlesex who showed strong signs of possession."

I wonder what these signs were—floating metres off the floor, perhaps? Moving objects around the room without touching them? Speaking in languages that haven't existed for hundreds to thousands of years?

"The most prominent symptom was a seizure that some may identify as epilepsy, but I was sure it was part of her possession."

I chuckle a little and shake my head. A few people glare in my direction. Poor people, they are actually buying this crap.

"In the end, we identified that she was possessed by the demon Ahriman, and we began the Catholic Rites of Exorcism on her."

I snort. This time, I do it too loud, and everyone turns to look at me. Even Dr Olivia Chase pauses her presentation because of my seemingly rude interruption, leaning her body weight onto one leg as she folds her arms.

"Is there a problem?"

I look around. She's definitely talking to me. I shrug.

"I assume you are a sceptic, yes?"

I sigh. "No, I am not a sceptic."

"No?"

"Not at all. I believe in demons. I've seen demons. Many times."

"I see. And yet you have a problem with the presentation?"

I hesitate. I know I should keep a low profile, but something about the intensity of her glare draws me in. She has a fuck you attitude that invites me into the confrontation.

"Yes, I do," I say.

"And what may that be, dare I ask?"

She asks the question in such a snooty, self-entitled manner that it makes me feel less guilty for what I'm about to do.

"Well, you say you identified the demon Ahriman in this girl, yes?"

"That is correct.

"And you say you used the Catholic Rites of Exorcism on her, yes?"

"That is also correct."

"And they worked?"

"Oh, absolutely. She ended up completely free of the demon."

I smile. Wonder how to articulate this. I want to soak up all the satisfaction I'm about to get.

"I'm confused, then," I say. "Mostly, about how those rites worked."

"Why would you be confused? They are the standard exorcism rites, and once we had the demon's name, we had enough power over it for it to work."

"I see. I'm just wondering how the Catholic Rites of Exorcism worked on a demon that doesn't come from Catholicism or any denomination of Christianity. You identified a demon from Zoroastrianism."

"Excuse me?"

"Zoroastrianism. It's an ancient religion that was prominent in the Middle East in about the seventh to sixth century BC before Islam came to Persia—now known as Iran—and eradicated it. It hasn't existed in the last two and a half thousand years."

"Yes, I know what Zoroastrianism is."

"Well, my issue is, that you say knowing the demon's name made the Catholic Rites of Exorcism work—but how would they work if the demon was from an entirely different religion with no links to Catholicism at all?"

She goes to answer, then doesn't. Everyone's eyes turn from me to her.

"If you had looked into Ahriam," I continued, "you would have discovered that Zoroastrians believed Ahriam to be the demon of all demons, the ultimate bad guy, and that he was a desert spirit. Considering he was a desert spirit, it makes me wonder what he would get out of possessing a girl in Middlesex."

Her mouth opens. She stutters over words.

"Honestly, there is no way that the demon that possessed that girl could have been Ahriam, or that your rites could have worked by knowing Ahriam's name when the demon is from an entirely different religion. And seeing as the major symptom this girl had was epileptic seizures, I suggest that any success your exorcism had would have been because of the placebo effect. Then again, I wonder whether doctors had started her on a course of medication to help with her epilepsy that happened to coincide with your exorcism, therefore eradicating the seizures at the same time. Might that be a possibility, Dr Chase?"

Silence.

Not a word.

She has nothing to say. No response to give. No answers to provide.

I sit back and watch as she stumbles through the rest of the presentation as if this never happened. By the time she's finished, half of the audience has walked out in disgust, and she avoids looking at me again.

Three

The winter evening is cool, but I don't mind the cold. I place my bag inside the compartment on my motorbike and wonder where I'm going to go next. Maybe I will find a hotel, or a bed-and-breakfast, or a field where I can sleep under the stars.

I take out my phone. April only texts me occasionally, but I still check, hopeful for a hint of where I may be of use; where I might find a case of demonic possession where the church refuses to intervene. Perhaps it would be bad press, or too much attention, or a clearly possessed victim will not meet their threshold of evidence—such as a case a few months ago where a boy levitated six feet off the ground, but the church decided not to intervene as he was a politician's son, and they feared the high-profile nature of the case might risk their ability to work in the shadows. When the Sensitives can't intervene, that's when I come in.

Sometimes, I pretend April doesn't only text me because she has another case for me. I convince myself it's because she's wanting to make sure I'm okay. Wanting to keep in touch.

But the text messages never begin with *how are you*. They begin with *Hi Mo we have a case for you.*

Today, however, there are no text messages. Just a screen of old messages and a dying battery. I place it in my pocket and mount my motorbike.

The distinct sound of high heels approach the car next to my motorbike. I glance over my shoulder.

It's her.

Her face falls the instant she sees me. She stops, shakes her head, and then proceeds to her car.

"It's you," she grunts.

I smile. "It certainly is."

She dumps her bag on her backseat and marches to the driver's door, but doesn't get in. Instead, she turns to me, leans back against the car, and folds her arms. Her blazer and trousers and cream-coloured blouse are pristine. Her hair is bottle blond and neat. Her makeup is subtly applied, red lipstick and foundation to cover blemishes. She looks almost too perfect.

"That was quite some stunt you pulled," she tells me, and it's hard to tell if she's impressed and angry, or just angry.

"It wasn't a stunt," I say, looking away from her. "It was the truth."

"The truth, huh?"

"Yes. I believe in what I do, and I don't like it when people give misinformation."

She curls her lip and shakes her head. I can't help but laugh a little; I'd feel sorry for humiliating her if she appeared in the least remorseful.

"Misinformation? I've studied demons for over a decade, you arrogant prick."

"And I've been on the battlefield fighting them, while you do your silly little imitations of an exorcism to people who need therapy rather than religious dogma."

"You think you're so right, don't you?"

I don't know whether there's any point to this. "I can see I'm evidently not going to change your mind. I think I'll go now."

I turn the ignition on my motorbike.

"I'll admit, you gave me a little to think about," she says, and I try to read her face, unable to tell whether she's being genuine, or whether this is another bout of resentful diatribe.

"A little?"

"What's your name, anyway?"

I sigh. "My name is Moses."

"Moses what?"

"Moses Iscariot."

"Iscariot? As in, descendant of–"

"Judas Iscariot, yes."

"So it's in your blood to be a backstabber?"

"That's if you believe Judas was a backstabber."

Most people don't know that Judas wrote a gospel that was omitted from the bible. Nor do they know an Egyptian antiques dealer in the 1970s found it and left it in a safe deposit box as the church denied its existence. And nor do they know that it was translated in 2000-2006, and that the translation told a very different story about my ancestor—a story where Judas helped to free Jesus from the constraints of his mortal body.

But I wouldn't expect a woman like this to know that, would I?

"Okay then, Mr Iscariot–"

"Please, just Mo."

"Okay, *Mo*—I'm about to go meet a man that claims to be possessed. How about you come along and give me your expert opinion?"

I frown. "Are you taking the piss?"

"No, I am not, as you so eloquently put, taking the piss. I am inviting you to meet a man who claims to be possessed, and to tell me what you think."

"You want my opinion?"

"I want to see if you're as good as you think you are."

I'm about to tell her to stick it up her arse, to say I'm not prepared to join her in meeting another false case, that I know it will just be pointless—but what she says next intrigues me.

"He's in prison."

"Prison?"

"Yes. His name is Billy Tate."

"I heard about that case on the news. Killed his wife and child, didn't he?"

"He certainly did."

"And you're going to visit him, why?"

"He claims he was possessed when he did it. Claims he has no recollection of it."

I snort back a laugh. "Of course he does. And you believe him?"

"I don't know whether I believe him, that is why I am going to visit him."

I hesitate. Look at my phone. It's hardly like I have any other cases on the go. And curiosity is truly getting the better of me.

"Fine," I say. "But don't play any stupid pop music or anything. I do classic rock only."

She frowns. "How about jazz?"

"Fine."

I take the keys from my motorbike and get into the passenger seat of her car. The air freshener is overwhelming, a lemon scent that makes me cough. My dirty boots feel out of place in the footrest. There's no filth anywhere, not even a line of dust on the dashboard.

She climbs into the driver's seat with an awkward elegance only intelligent people have, and I hate to admit that it's a little endearing. She turns the ignition and backs out of the spot so slowly that we're barely moving. I can already tell I'm going to hate her driving.

Billy Speaks

Scuttle scuttle scuttle.

A beetle climbs the cold, stone walls.

My finger traces its route, up the bumpy rock, past the barred window, higher and higher until I'm on tippytoes atop the flat mattress of my metal bed.

I take the beetle.

Hold it high.

Squeeze it between my fingers.

Its legs wiggle. Like they are running. Like it's trying to escape. But there's nowhere to scuttle, my little friend, there's nowhere at all.

I reach out my tongue. Lower it.

Its little legs scramble across the tip of my pink flesh, barely scraping the spongy surface.

I place it between my incisors. Hold it there. Squeeze as its legs run, wiggle, frantic, oh so frantic, and I push my teeth down and it collapses under the strength and its body squeezes and it splatters as it cracks and breaks.

I chew. Munch. Swallow.

Now the beetle is inside of me.

"What the fuck are you doing, you freak?"

I turn. Over my shoulder. Another voice. Another face. Big. Beefy. Tattoos. So many tattoos. Everyone has tattoos in here. Tribal decorations suited to our ancestors cover the bulky muscles of men who wasted their life like it was nothing.

Sometimes I hear them. Sometimes I don't.

But there's always something inside of me listening.

Prying.

Anticipating.

Always inside of me, sitting in the waiting room, listening through the wall to hear what's going on, ready to burst in when the moment arrives.

It eats the beetles.

Not me.

That wasn't me.

It was the thing inside of me.

Sometimes I just can't tell who's in control.

"Oi, I asked you a fucking question."

I turn. Greasy hair flops over my face. Not had a shower in days. Oily strands tangle into spikes that hang over my left eye. Like prison bars over my vision.

He stands in the doorway to our cell.

"I swear, I fucking hate sharing this cell with you." He slumps down on his bed and leans back, holding a tatty book in front of him; something meant for children that he struggles to read.

I watch him. Study him. Consume his imperfections. Take in his aggressive aura. Everything he is, Billy is not.

"Stop fucking staring at me," he says. "Stop it or I'll break your fucking neck."

I shake my head. I'm back. It's gone, and I'm here. And I am watching this man, and I don't know why I'm watching him, a murderer who could break me in half, who could grind my bones like they are ash, and I am suddenly terrified, arms shake, knees quiver—what am I doing in here?

"I'm sorry," I say, and I abruptly lie back on my hard bed. "I'm sorry."

I repeat it to make sure he does not hurt me.

He scoffs and mumbles something under his breath.

There is a taste in my mouth and I don't know what it is. It's sour. Rotten.

I look around the cell.

I keep blacking out. I keep forgetting.

I am confined by these four walls and I don't remember getting here.

I recall the words they said at the trial. My family. Murdered. Dead.

But I don't understand.

How could they be dead? How could I have killed them? How could I have hurt the family I love so much?

Because you're a monster, Billy.

It's back.

The voice.

Again.

I look at my cellmate. He doesn't react. I look around. Maybe it's whispering at me through the pipes. Maybe it's outside my cell. Maybe it's my shadow.

I don't know where it is, but it's always somewhere behind me, and I wish it would stop.

Being in here terrifies me. The voice terrifies me even more.

We're in this together, Billy.

Shut up.

Go away.

I don't know you.

We're going to hurt him, Billy.

Hurt who?

Him.

Who?

He called you a freak, Billy. He had the audacity to call you a freak.

Who did?

My head turns. I don't move it, but it turns. And it directs my eyes toward my cellmate.

It's what he deserves, Billy.

What does he deserve?

Stop being naïve, Billy.

Naïve?

We are in this together, Billy.

In what together?

I don't understand.

I don't understand any of this.

Relax, Billy. Relax. I've got you.

My eyelids droop. I am tired. I didn't feel it, but I am now. My head falls back. My consciousness wavers. I fall into a sleepless slumber. The kind where the world is distant, and all I have are my empty thoughts.

I feel myself fall.

I feel my arms rise.

Hours pass, but they feel like minutes.

I taste something in my mouth.

It's thick.

Coppery.

There is screaming.

When I open my eyes, there is screaming.

Darkness.

I am awake. I've been awake for a while. I don't understand how I've been awake, but I am awake. I wasn't aware. I wasn't aware of any of this.

Something flings me around. Like a rag doll. My legs wavering. Flying.

There is something between my teeth.

Skin.

His skin.

My cellmate's skin.

Well done, Billy. You're making us both proud.

My teeth are clamping down on his skin, the space between his shoulder and his neck, and blood is pouring down my chin, and he is screaming, and I am screaming though it's muffled, and there is a commotion behind me, and there are hands on my body and my shoulders and they want to pull me but they can't, my teeth have clamped down too hard, and they are shouting at me to stop and I don't know how to stop and I don't know how to let go and I don't know what to do.

Keep going, Billy. Keep biting. Sink those teeth in further. Sink them right in. Taste the blood.

A fist to my belly winds me, and my bite loosens, and they pull me, and it's their opportunity, they grab me, take me off, and they throw me to the floor, a group of them pinning me to the ground, one on my legs, one on my back, another with my arms behind my back.

I can't breathe and I don't know what's happening.

He's shouting.

My cellmate. He's shouting.

It's full of profanities. Full of hostility. He's furious. He's being restrained. Someone with gloves presses down on the wound. The blood is over the floor. Over the bedsheets. Over my chin.

How beautiful does that taste, Billy?

I don't know who you are. How you are doing this. Why you keep talking to me. Stop it. I don't want you here. Leave me alone.

Leave you alone?

Yes. Go. Now. I don't want this.

But we've come so far, Billy.

All you do is torture me.

Am I crazy?

Who am I even talking to right now?

Myself?

I wasn't you before, but I am now, Billy. We are one. Together.

Please, leave me alone.

We've come this far, Billy.

I don't want you here.

Relax, Billy. Just relax. Sink back and let me take over. I'll deal with the screws.

No, you'll hurt them.

One of them leans too hard on my back. It hurts.

I'll take care of them, Billy.

I try to resist, but it hurts too much, and I want it to stop.

I'll make it stop, Billy.

It's too painful. I need it to end. I need him to get off.

I'll make him get off, Billy.

Fine. End the pain. Just this once.

Thank you, Billy. You know I'll take care of you.

I close my eyes. Sink back. Suddenly, I feel nothing. I'm distant. Somewhere else.

I wonder what will have happened when I wake up.

Four

I can tell having the window down irritates her. Being honest, I only intended to have it down for a few minutes to give me a bit of air—but, seeing as she keeps aiming passive aggressive glances in my direction, I find myself leaving it open.

I was right about her driving. As soon as she gets onto the motorway, she finds the middle lane and stays there. If I was in another car, I'd be raging at her—she's disrupting the traffic and getting undertaken over and over—but she seems completely oblivious.

Once she leaves the motorway and I can stop feeling embarrassed by the glares other drivers give us as they pass, I turn to get a better look at her. I'm impressed by how she can use the pedals with such huge high heels on. She frowns when she's concentrating. She looks impressive in her suit, though—she is what April would refer to as a 'power woman' and, whilst most men would feel intimidated by such a woman, I can't help but be saddened that she feels she must wear masculine clothes to be taken seriously.

I try to guess at how old she is, but it's hard to tell behind that much makeup. I reckon early thirties, but she may be older.

"So how long have you been doing this?" she asks, breaking the long-lasting silence I was enjoying. "Studying demons, I mean."

"I wouldn't say I study them."

"Fighting them, then."

I shrug. "Years. Who knows? I found out I was a Sensitive when they recruited me."

"A sensitive—I've not heard of that. What is it?"

I'm torn between a knowing smile and an aggravated grimace. One would have thought someone who studies demonology would know of the Sensitives, but then again, it shows how well the secret is kept. It is sad, however, that the Sensitives saved the world a few years ago, stopping Hell from unleashing a tirade of demons upon the world, ensuring that the world's population could continue with their lives, blissfully unaware of what could have been—yet she has no idea.

"A Sensitive is someone who's sensitive to the paranormal. Who can pick up on the presence of demons. Someone who's born with a gift."

"How are they born with it? Just a talent? I don't believe in that stuff."

"It's not a talent—we have the ability because Heaven conceived us, much like Jesus."

She laughs. "So you're telling me there's a bunch of messiahs walking around?"

"Not messiahs. Just ordinary people with the power to do something the rest of the world will never appreciate."

A silence lingers between us. I can feel her making a choice, much like I am—a choice between whether to engage in an argument about this, or whether to let it go.

She chooses to let it go.

"How many exorcisms would you have said you've done?"

I shrug. "A lot. Nearly a hundred, maybe. You?"

"About the same."

"And out of all those exorcisms—how many were genuinely possessed?"

"All of them."

"What, like the woman you showed in the presentation?"

"And how exactly are you so sure all the exorcisms you've done were genuine?"

"I felt it."

"You felt it?"

"Yes."

She chuckles.

I'm tempted to tell her about all the other ways I was sure—the victim levitating high above the bed, speaking in languages that have long since died out, moving objects around the room without touching them, forcing huge gusts to push me against the wall of a room with closed windows. But those are just ways of confirming what I already know—my best indication of possession is my gut.

And I don't feel like I need to justify myself to her.

We continue the last ten minutes in silence until she turns down a narrow road. Either side of the road are signs saying things such as *Smuggling in Contraband? Think Again!* and *Giving Drugs to a Prisoner? You May End Up Joining Them!* Eventually, she pulls into a car park and comes to a stop, parking far too close to the left of the parking space.

We step out. She straightens her jacket. Uncreases her blouse. Pats down her trousers. I follow her to the prison entrance. She struggles to walk properly in heels, kind of lopsided, like she's always falling forward, and I wish she'd wear some proper shoes.

A prison officer greets us with a glum expression—he is clearly a man who does not enjoy his job. He makes us surrender our mobile phones and step through a metal detector. Then they search us—every pocket, every fold in our clothes, beneath our tongue, beneath the strands of our hair.

The prison officer eyes me up and down once he finds nothing, and for a second, I think he's going to insist on a more intimate search. As it is, he lets us through, and we pause at a desk where an older, even more jaded prison officer scowls at us. He's overweight and pale. I heard that a prison officer's average life expectancy is shorter than most, and this guy looks like he's close to the end.

"We have an appointment to see Billy Tate," Olivia tells him.

He sighs, looks at the computer screen, and clicks the mouse a few times.

"I am Dr Olivia Chase," she tells him, as if knowing she has a PhD will make him cooperate.

After a while, he stops clicking and turns his scowl toward us.

"The visitation is denied," he says.

We await further information, but none is forthcoming.

"Excuse me?" Olivia says. "What do you mean, visitation is denied?"

"I mean, visitation is denied. He's not allowed any visitors."

"Why not?"

The prison officer huffs and clicks the mouse a few more times.

"He attacked his cellmate," he says. "He's in solitary."

"But we have travelled quite a distance."

"I'm sure you have."

"When will we be allowed to see him?"

The prison officer shrugs.

"This is ridiculous! You don't think you could have called us? We have had this meeting scheduled for a while."

He shrugs again.

"I insist you let him see us."

The prison officer smirks.

"Hey, Olivia," I say, pulling her away from the irritating man.

"What?" she snaps.

"Just wait here for a minute," I tell her. "I'll sort it."

"What do you mean, you'll sort it?"

I don't reply. Instead, I retreat through the entrance and collect my mobile phone. I dial April's number and put the phone to my ear.

"Mo?" she says. She sounds happy to hear from me.

"Hey, April."

"How are you? It's been ages."

"It has. I'm good. Listen, I need a favour—do you think you could get the Church to help?"

She says yes and I explain the situation to her. As we wait for the Church to intervene, she asks me how I am. It feels good talking to her. I miss her. It's almost as if it isn't painful to hear her voice.

I return to Olivia a few minutes later.

"Try again," I tell her.

Confused, she approaches the prison officer. Just as he's about to deny us again, the prison warden appears from a room behind him, leers at us, then whispers something in the prison officer's ear.

The prison officer—who appears grumpy—says, "Visitation granted," and leads us to the visitation room.

Five

The visitation room is one of the most depressing rooms I've ever been in.

It's full of round tables and metal chairs, all screwed to the solid floor. The visitors sitting at these tables look miserable, each waiting for their inmate to arrive whilst wearing an absent glare—parents, friends, families, all looking down, or at the wall, or at their lap; anywhere but each other. There is a machine with chocolates and crisps in the corner where you can buy gifts for your prisoner, and every now and then, someone limps over to it and grumbles about how expensive it is as they rest their change in their palm, sifting through coins to find enough to give their loved one a poor reprieve from a long sentence of misery.

Every few minutes, a prison officer brings another inmate out and places them at a table. There is occasionally a sad, despairing hug that the prison officer quickly stops. Then they sit and stare at their family as unspoken guilt passes between them. They engage in small talk like strangers at a bus stop, trying to pretend there is something normal about this situation.

The inmates wear their own clothes, which I wasn't expecting. Most of them are in tatty tracksuit bottoms and plain t-shirts, sometimes with a rip or stain. One has a web tattoo on their neck, but most look like any normal person you might encounter in the street. For all I know, these people could be the people serving me in the bank, or cutting my hair in the barbers, or doing the accounts for some rich guy. It makes me wonder how many criminals I've met without knowing it.

After they have brought four or five inmates out, the prison officer guides a young man through. Probably late twenties. Quite small. A hunched, non-threatening demeanour. He is the only one with restraints on, has his wrists and ankles shackled in front of his waist, and he is forced to hobble in with limited movement.

Olivia waves her arm. "Over here."

The prison officer guides him over to us. Olivia stands, so I do the same. She offers a hand which Billy takes, giving her a meek, limp handshake.

"Hello, Billy, it's lovely to see you," she says. "This is my colleague, Mr Moses Iscariot."

"Call me Mo," I say. I don't offer my hand, and neither does Billy.

"Please, sit," Olivia says, and we retake our seats as Billy sits opposite.

There is an uncomfortable silence as he glances from her, to me, then back to her. He keeps his head bowed slightly and struggles to make eye contact with either of us.

"Oh, I'm sorry, would you like some chocolate?" she asks. "I can get you some from the machine."

He considers this, then gives a faint shake of his head.

"How are you finding things here?" she asks.

He opens his mouth to reply, then responds with a shrug.

"We understand your lawyers are planning to plead not guilty by reason of insanity, is that right?"

He neither shakes nor nods his head. Instead, he just stares forward. Some may see this as a stoic resistance, but I can tell he's fighting back tears.

"And what have your lawyers said?"

Billy doesn't reply.

"Billy," I say, wondering if maybe Olivia's interrogation-style questioning isn't helping. "Why don't you tell us how you are? Honestly."

He opens his mouth, but still nothing comes out.

"You can tell us the truth. We're here to help, not judge."

Finally, he speaks. "Not... good..."

"Not good?" I repeat. "In what way?"

"I... My inmate... They say I hurt him, but I don't—I don't remember..."

"Why don't you remember, Billy?"

He shrugs.

"Did you blackout?" I ask.

He nods.

I try to engage my feelings; to see what my gut is telling me about him. I try to listen to what I can sense from this guy. I need him to look at me, I need to hold his gaze, as it feels like whatever's in there is buried deep, and I can't quite get a handle on it.

"Is that what happened the night your family died, Billy?" I ask.

Now he looks up at me. His eyes are wide, fixed on mine, fully dilated. A hollow stare. His lip quivers, and his arms tremble, but there is a distant fire in those pupils, hidden behind his vulnerability. He is weak, but there is something strong within him, something far stronger than he is—and it is not a part of him.

I don't know who or what it is yet, but it is not him.

And I decide that I believe him.

"I know you didn't kill them, Billy," I say.

His eyes water, but he fights it. He shakes more. His whole body convulses. Olivia looks at me, concerned, worried that Billy might explode—but this is what we need; we need him tense; scared; angry; we need it to show itself so we can see it.

"I know you didn't," I say. "But something inside of you did."

"I think what Mo is trying to say–" Olivia tries, but I interrupt her; this isn't the time for her make-believe demons, this is the time for Billy's truth.

"There is something inside of you, isn't there? Something that talks to you. But I don't think you know what it is. Do you?"

Billy's breath quickens. He's panting. His fingers grip his trousers, curling up the fabric in his fists.

"Why don't you tell us what you do know about it?"

Billy looks around. At the other inmates with their families. With their friends. All so normal compared to him. "It talks to me," he says, his voice little more than a whisper.

"What do you mean?"

"It talks to me. Tells me things. I can talk back to it."

"And when it talks to you, where is it?"

"What do you mean?"

"Is it inside of your head, or outside?"

"... Both. Sometimes it whispers in my ear, sometimes it shouts, sometimes it's at the back of my mind, sometimes it's across the room, I can't—I can't ever tell..."

"That's okay, Billy. You're doing really well."

"My lawyer says I should plead insanity. But I don't feel insane."

"That's because you're not insane, Billy."

"But my family, how could I..."

"You didn't."

"He says I did. He says *we* did."

I realise Olivia is staring at me. Transfixed. I can't tell if it's admiration or resentment. Maybe it's neither.

"What else has it made you do?"

"My... my cell mate... I opened my eyes, and there was blood..."

I put my hand on the table.

"Give me your hand, Billy."

"What?"

"I said give me your hand."

I need to touch his skin; I need to know how it feels; I need to sense its presence; feel its rage—I need to find out what we're dealing with.

Billy reluctantly places his hand on the table.

I place mine on top of it. I close my eyes.

It's strong.

If it was new, only just entered his body, I'd be able to tell, but this is embedded in Billy, latched onto his soul. It has a firm grip, and its claws are digging in.

Mr Iscariot...

I hear it.

Inside.

Billy looks at me. Our eyes meet. He can hear it too. It speaks to both of us.

You are not welcome here...

"Let him go."

Make me...

"There is nothing more you can get from him. Just let him go."

It cackles.

Olivia stares at me, caught somewhere between intrigue and outrage.

But I can hear it. I know it's there.

How's your Daddy...

Dear old Daddy...
I see him in Hell sometimes...
I see him...
And I fuck his eternal soul until he cries...
That's right...
The big bad man cries...

"Ow!" Billy snatches his hand away.

I didn't realise I was gripping so hard.

"What are you doing?" Olivia asks.

I just look at her. Then to Billy. Dumbfounded.

No demon has ever done that before.

No demon has ever spoken to me so clearly.

No demon has ever wielded power over me before I've even begun to fight it.

I want to know more. I need to know more.

I grab Billy's hands. He tries to release it, but I don't let him. I grab it; I want to hear more; I want to know more; I want this fucker to try taunting me again; go on you piece of shit, give me your worst...

"Mo, stop it!"

I ignore Olivia. Keep gripping. Keep ignoring Billy's struggles.

"Moses—Mr Iscariot—please!"

"Oi, no touching!" The prison officer shouts across the room, and heads turn, but I do not let go.

"Come on," I tell it. "You were so cocky a second ago. Why don't you come at me again? Huh? Why don't you?"

The prison officer comes over, grabs my collar, shoves me off, then hoists Billy up by the arm and drags him away.

"No, please, we're not finished–"

The prison officer ignores Olivia.

Billy keeps his eyes on mine until he leaves.

The prison officer returns moments later to tell us to leave.

"Well done!" Olivia says as we collect our phones and head

for the exit. "You absolute imbecile! How are we meant to help him now?"

She thinks she knows. Thinks she's right. Thinks she has reason to be on her high horse.

But she doesn't know.

Truly, honestly, she does not know what she's dealing with. Not even a bit.

She does not have a clue.

Six

She drives in silence.

I'd be grateful, except it's not empty silence. She punctuates every minute that passes with another huff. Another shake of her head. Another glance at the window at the fields rushing past. She's seething, and though she says nothing, she makes sure I know.

My dad used to be angry at me all the time, except he'd never force me to endure passive aggressive exhalations; he'd let me know with his fists. My face may not be bruised from Olivia's knuckles, but her feelings are wounded just the same.

Me, I'm not bothered. I'm used to being the fuck up. I've had it for thirty-six years. Still, I can't help it—I bite, if only to see what she's clearly so desperate to say.

"Why don't you just spit it out?"

"Spit what out?"

"Whatever it is you're thinking."

"And what makes you so sure I'm thinking something?"

I raise my eyebrows and look at her. She goes to object, then seems to decide that she'd rather let me have it.

"Fine. I regret ever asking you to come along on this case."

I laugh.

I don't intend to be antagonistic, it's just an involuntary reaction.

Still, it doesn't break her stride.

"I regret the moment you entered my lecture theatre and made me look like a fool. I regret when you told me about this Sensitive nonsense. I regret when I let you intervene with whoever it was you called."

"Anything else?"

"Yes, and I—I... I regret letting you in my car."

I laugh again. This time louder. Again, unintentionally, but this rant is so obscenely amusing.

"Rightyo, Olivia."

"It's Dr Chase."

"Barely."

"Excuse me?"

"Tell you what—you try doing this without my help."

"Oh, you think I can't perform an exorcism without you?"

"No, I don't. But most of all, I don't think you stand a damned chance in hell of getting close to that man without some serious pull—and I just don't think you have the contacts to make it happen."

She shakes her head. Goes to deny what I've just said, but can't, so instead comes out with, "Yes, well I wouldn't have had an issue if it wasn't for your escapades!"

"Escapades?"

"Yes!"

"Now that's a fancy word. I guess that's what a PhD gives you, after all."

She goes to argue again, but instead grunts at me and continues driving in her heated silence, fuming at whatever story she's concocting in her mind.

Sometimes, I do this too. Someone annoys me, so I tell

myself a story about what they've done, then another one, then another, and before I know it, I'm living in a reality where this person is the worst human to grace this earth.

I did it with the love of April's life—the reason she would never be with me. Until, one day, I realised he wasn't the bad guy I'd made him out to be in the stories I told myself. I realised that, perhaps, it was me who was the arsehole.

"Listen, I'm sorry if I–"

She puts her hand up to form a barrier between us, and any notion of an olive branch I was to offer ceases.

Fuck it, maybe this is a good idea. Maybe I could leave this case to her and have a break. Carry on wandering the country, aimless as a leaf on the breeze, going wherever I happen to turn the wheel of my bike. I'll sleep under the stars and wonder if there are many other worlds out there with a Hell desperate to destroy it.

She can sort out Billy Tate.

She can fight the demon that is way too powerful for her to even comprehend.

She can take this case on, and I can carry on being alone and miserable. The way I like it. It's the best I can do.

Then I remember it's not just her that will suffer. It's not just Dr Olivia 'Charlatan' Chase. It's a man who is facing life in prison for a murder he doesn't remember committing. A man who is suffering alone in a prison cell, doomed to mental torment, spiralling deeper and deeper under the control of whatever creature is clutching onto his soul.

I can't get my handle on what kind of demon it is. Normally, I can touch the person and feel the demon—I can see its true form and find out its name—but this demon is able to resist, and it wounds my ego. Even so, I could let my pride go if it weren't for the knowledge of the constant suffering that man will be enduring.

She pulls up outside the university. Turns toward the window and rests her chin on her fist. Waits for me to leave.

I don't.

"Listen—" I try.

"Just go."

"No."

She turns to me. Eyes like a lion. Nose curled. Face fierce like a warrioress.

"You know you won't be able to get back in that prison," I tell her. "You know you can't arrange another meeting with Billy without me. And you know I will go back and help that man whether or not you choose to tag along. If you want to be involved in this case, you need me."

She says nothing.

But I can see it in her expression.

Realisation sinking in. The awareness that I'm correct. The self-resentment for having to admit it.

I open her glove compartment. She scowls at me. I find a scrap of paper. A receipt of some kind. I reach further in and there's a pen. I have to scribble it against the back of the receipt, but eventually it works. I write my phone number on the receipt and place it in the drinks compartment beside the handbrake.

"That's my number," I tell her. "Book another appointment with Billy in the morning. I'll make sure it will be approved—then text me the time to meet you."

She doesn't look at me, but she looks at the receipt I leave between us.

I open the door, pause, then turn back to her.

"I really do think you have potential, you know," I tell her, and I'm sure I see a smile that she quickly disguises.

I get out of the car and trudge back to my motorbike. I text April to ask her to speak to the Church; to ensure that Olivia's request is approved.

By the time I put my helmet on, start the ignition, and glance at my mobile phone, the battery almost dead, I have a response saying it has been done.

Billy Speaks

Two interesting people.
   Two interesting cases.
   He knows. He's full of it. He thinks he can remove me from our body. He is aware of his gift, his power. He is a Sensitive.
   His arrogance is his weakness, and his father is his downfall.
   But her...
   I didn't look at her. Deliberately didn't meet her eyes.
   Because I don't want her to know.
   At the moment, she has no idea.
   But I do...
   I know what she is...
   I'm led between the cells. A screw has his hand on my back. I find it hard to remember where I've been.
   But there are glimpses.
   Always glimpses.
   A man. A woman.
   I think they are here to help me.
   Misguided fools, Billy.
   Silly, silly people.

Wannabe heroes.

They think they will help, but they have no idea that they will only make me stronger.

Other inmates glance at me as I pass. They wander the cell block, being given the luxury of a little time out of their cells. Many of them back away from me. Retreat upon knowing what I did to their friend. Some stand their ground. Leer at me as I pass. Draw a line across their neck with their finger. Promise retribution.

Occasionally, one steps forward. The screw holds his arm out to back the inmate off.

They speak to me.

The same promises over and over.

"You're dead."

"I'll fucking kill you."

"Just you wait, you fucking prick."

I miss my family.

I miss my wife.

I miss my child.

I shouldn't be here. I'm not one of them. This isn't right.

Give it time, Billy. Give it time.

We'll be out of here soon enough.

When it's the right moment.

I need to know first.

I need to know.

Need to know what?

And how are we getting out of here?

Please tell me you're not going to hurt anyone.

Relax. Sit back. Enjoy the show.

You won't get to see it for much longer.

Please, no. Just leave them be. Just leave me be. Leave everyone be.

Quiet, Billy. You know nothing. Sit in your corner and shut up.

They open my cell. A single-person cell. It's a new one. My few books and notepads are in a box on the rough mattress.

I get a cell all to myself because I attacked another inmate, and they will hate me for it.

I'm really sure that someone will kill me in here.

I wouldn't let them, Billy.

I would break their necks before they could touch you.

I'd snap their muscles and grind their bones and use their spine to play their tendons like a violin.

Please don't hurt anyone.

We'll be out of here soon, Billy. Just be quiet until then.

I have thoughts to ponder.

Conundrums to entertain.

A woman to analyse...

A woman?

The woman who saw me.

They are trying to help me. Leave them alone.

They are trying to tear us apart, Billy.

Don't you see?

They mock us. They wish to separate us. But they won't manage, Billy, they won't manage.

Because they don't know who she is.

Who she is?

I see Heaven in him. He's a child of all that is pure. He's flawed but honourable. He will do what he believes is the right thing.

She will ruin that.

She has no idea what fire burns within her soul.

I don't understand.

You don't need to.

Soon, it will be just me.

Your pain will end.

You will be gone.

I don't want to go.

This is my body.

This is my life.

But it's not your soul.

Not anymore

It's mine

I'm squeezing it right now—can you feel it? I'm sinking my teeth into it and it tastes like strawberries and liquorice.

Soon, it will taste like tar and burnt meat.

I hear them howling. Taunting me through the walls.

I don't know what's worse, the threats from the prisoners or the voice in my head.

She does not know.

Olivia Chase.

She does not know.

Know what?

Why are you obsessing over this woman?

What is it you're so desperate to do to her?

Do to her?

Oh, Billy.

It is not what I can do to her...

It is what she can do for us.

I will kill all of them, Billy. Every inmate in here. Every screw who stands in our way. We will run from here and feed on every soul we need to give us energy.

Then she will unleash the very worst Hell has to imagine.

I don't understand.

What are you on about?

You needn't worry, Billy.

You are but a pawn.

I am but a prince.

And now we've found her, we've found our queen.

It won't be long now, Billy.

Then it will all be quiet for you, and everyone else will hear the screams.

Just a little time, Billy.
Just a little time.

BEFORE

Seven

Grey clouds and early evening darkness cannot spoil Billy's mood. Nor can they dampen Jennifer's spirits in the car beside him, or their daughter's excitement in the backseat.

They are going to the theatre.

To her first pantomime.

They'd watched one on television last year—the ones they always show on ITV2, usually full of a cast of people who used to be celebrities that make you say "I didn't know they were still alive."

And she has been looking forward to it all year, ever since they promised they'd take her.

"And do you think Jasmine will be there? And that Genie will be there? And that Aladdin will have the lamp and everything?"

He smiles at her in the rear-view mirror.

"I guess we'll just have to find out."

She bounces in her car seat, the one she's almost outgrown. Oh, how quickly time passes. All those times he saved his tears for when his wife was asleep, begrudging another negative pregnancy test, another fertility test, another year gone by without a child. It was tough.

Yet there she is.

Their little miracle.

"What are you smiling about?"

He glances at Jennifer. He hadn't realised he'd been smiling so widely.

"Oh, nothing," he says. "I'm just happy."

She places a hand on his leg and gives it a gentle squeeze.

"Dad!"

"What is it?"

"I dropped Damien."

"I'll get it," Jennifer says, and reaches her hand behind her seat. Her face ends up next to his shoulder, and she stares at Billy as she moves her hand around the floor, searching for the leg of Tilly's teddy.

"I can't find it," she says. "Where did it drop, Tilly?"

"Just beneath the chair."

She reaches further, which presses her face harder against his shoulder.

"No, I can't find it."

"Here, I can probably reach it," Billy suggests.

She pulls away and Billy, keeping his eyes on the road and one hand on the steering wheel, reaches his other arm beneath the seat and stretches, rotating his fingers back and forth in the hope of finding something furry.

His fingers stroke it.

"Ah, almost got it."

For a moment, he concentrates on keeping the car from veering. They are on a straight bit of road on an unlit estate. They are almost there, and he could easily say to Tilly that she should wait—but they have had so many problems with this bear that he can't bring himself to. It is her crux. Her safety.

The only thing that seems to quell her anxiety. Without it, the last ten minutes of the journey would be hell.

He reaches the teddy's leg and wraps his hand around it, but it falls out of reach again.

"Nearly there..."

He reaches his hand further and, for a fleeting moment, his head lowers beneath the dashboard and he doesn't see what's on the tarmac in front of him.

"Billy!" his wife screams.

Her panic makes him slam on the brakes. He retracts his arm and returns his focus to the windscreen—at a figure in the middle of the road—and he can't brake hard enough or quick enough.

The car skids.

Twisting to the side, the brakes grinding as he presses hard on the pedal, and the vehicle comes to a stop just beside the silhouette of a crouched figure.

He stays still.

His hands gripping the wheel.

His wide eyes focussed on the outline in front of him.

Panting.

Sweating.

Tilly cries. Jennifer turns around and places a hand on Tilly's. She speaks words of comfort. Billy doesn't hear them. He's too engrossed with the person in the middle of the road.

Whoever it is, they don't look well.

"Stay in the car," he says. Undoes his seatbelt. Steps out of the car. Closes the door behind him.

And he approaches the silhouette.

The closer he gets, the clearer the outline of a young woman becomes, and the more her smell attacks him. She reeks of body odour. And rotting. And expired fruit.

He steps forward slowly. Cautiously. Putting a hand out in front of him as if he was calming an animal.

"Hey," he says, quietly and calmly. "Are you okay?"

Her face twists toward him, and her features become clearer in the headlights of the car: her muddy visage; her yellow teeth; her mucky, raggedy nightgown crusted with dirt; her filthy fingernails. Her hair is thick with a dark red substance. There are wounds up her arms, like someone has dragged claws up her skin; some have scabbed over, and some still glisten in the moonlight.

There is blood on the palm of her hands.

He crouches beside her, leaving a few feet between them, careful not to seem threatening.

"Are you all right?"

She shakes. Possibly from cold. Possibly from fright. Possibly from fury.

Who is this girl?

"My name is Billy," he says. "Billy Tate. What's yours?"

She looks up at him, then turns away, like he's a dangerous predator and she can't bear to look at him. She twitches, sudden jolts of movement, her eyes constantly wide, rubbing her hands up and down her bare arms.

She flexes her fingers and drags her nails across her skin.

"Hey, don't do that," Billy says, instinctively reaching out to pull her hand away. She is deadly cold. She flinches, and he retracts his hand.

"Is everything okay?" Jennifer calls, half stepping out of the car.

"Yes, fine," he calls back. "Stay in the car. Perhaps call..."

Not wanting to alarm the girl, he mouths *phone 999* at his wife, showing nine fingers to help to convey his request—as if this girl will not be able to figure it out.

He turns back to her. She is shaking even more furiously. She half looks at him, peering between greasy strands of her.

"Would you like my coat?" he asks. "You're shivering, would you like it?"

She doesn't answer.

Just shakes.

He takes off his coat and offers it to her, and she recoils away. As she does, her soiled nightie rides up her thigh, and he notices that something has been carved into her. It looks like a crucifix, except upside down.

"Please let me help you," Billy says. "You obviously aren't in a good way."

He glances over his shoulder to see if Jennifer is ringing the police. She has the phone by her ear.

He turns back to the girl. Moves closer. Notices more cuts on her thigh, just the same. They are fresh, some of them still bleeding.

"Who did that to you?" he asks.

She glances down at the cuts. Stares at them. Doesn't try to cover them up. Then looks back up at Billy. Scared. Sorrowful. Suffering.

He reaches his arm toward her and says, "Please let me help you. I will help you in any way I can."

Her eyebrows raise. Her vulnerability becomes more intense. She whispers, "Really?"

Billy nods. "Of course."

"Any way you can?" she repeats, her voice hoarse and quiet.

"Yes."

She pushes herself to her knees. Stares intently at her saviour. Edges closer to him.

Billy stays still, unsure what she is doing, remaining wary, remaining calm, reminding himself that this is a girl and not a rabid beast.

She kneels in front of him. Faces him. Looks up at him. Reaches her arms toward him.

She takes a deep breath.

She meets his kind, wise eyes with her bloodshot pupils.

And she whispers, "I'm sorry."

Before Billy can ask what for, her fingers are pressing against his temples, hard, and he feels a shot of excruciating pain shoot through his skull.

She leaps upon him.

Takes him to the ground.

Mounts him.

Opens her mouth. Wide. It stretches far more than a person's mouth should stretch. She places it over his, completely over, until her mouth is wrapped so tightly over his lips she's practically sucking his face into hers.

And she screams into him.

Billy's body seizes. Pain fires through his muscles. The world disappears.

When Billy's eyes open, there are paramedics over him.

He does not know what's happened. Where the girl is. What's going on.

He's lying on the road.

There are flashing lights.

His eyes move back and forth. There are ambulance and police. A crowd. Jennifer and Tilly across the road. Mother shielding her daughter from the sight, despite being unable to look away herself.

"He's conscious!" someone shouts.

He tries to sit up.

"Please, Mr Tate, stay where you are, you might be concussed."

Concussed?

From what?

He moves his back. Tries to get up. A burning sensation fires through his spine. He remains lying down, whimpering from the agony, and twists his head to the side.

And he sees the girl. Across the road. Sitting in the back of an ambulance.

She has handcuffs on.

A police officer stands next to her as a paramedic shines a light in her eyes.

She does not take her stare away from Billy.

Why is she in handcuffs? What did she do? Who is she?

Something feels strange.

In his head. He can't say what. He doesn't feel quite like himself.

It feels like there are hands inside his skull, squeezing his brain, squeezing it tighter, tighter, digging fingernails into cells. Like there is something large in his stomach, making him feel sick and hungry, swirling around, biting at his innards. Like something is swimming through his muscles, each one tightening, spasming, out of his control.

The paramedic says things. He doesn't hear them. Perhaps they have an explanation. Perhaps not.

He looks past them, ignoring whatever they are doing to him, and meets the girl's gaze.

And he stares. Unable to look away.

NOW

Eight

Darkness always feels thicker in a graveyard.

The moon is full, partially concealed by thick streaks of cloud that journey slowly past it. The night is still, with a slight breeze that nudges a wayward crisp packet across the ground, and a coldness that stiffens my fingers.

I step across the grass, frosted blades crunching beneath my boots. Some graves are thick with moss, letters engraved into the older stone almost indecipherable, once meaningful epitaphs forgotten by families who have either died or moved on. As one moves past the ageing slabs, they come across the newer plots, the fresher graves, the ones with families that still care enough to leave flowers and, on some tragic mounds of grass, teddy bears.

Dad's grave is the fourth one along on the third row.

The plant I left on this day last year is still here, only now it's brown, thick, and dead. The pot has crusted; the plastic becoming brittle as decay takes it over.

It reminds me how no one else cares about this one small piece of remembrance among hundreds of others.

I'm not sure how much I care anymore.

I drop my head. Shake my head. That's a lie. I do care. I'm just not sure why.

There were two sides to my father, each as distinct and different as summer and winter. There was the side of him that would take me for rides in his favourite car, that would tell me about all the old music he loved, that would share his philosophies and life lessons and musings and thoughts, that would aim to impart wisdom that might help guide me through the treacherous trail of life.

Then there was the other side. The one that wasn't so good. The one he constantly regretted yet still allowed to surface. It was the side of him that resented me for the death his wife while giving birth to me. The side that called me Killer. The side that drank until his fists swung for me, then drank some more, until the poison made him pass out and I could finally escape those fists as I fled the house.

I'd hang around on the green nearby. Watching other boys play football or ride their bikes. They never invited me to play. They didn't even tease me for being on my own. They never even acknowledged I was there. They were too apathetic toward my existence to bully me.

I'd return later, and Dad would still be passed out, usually on the sofa, his arm hanging over the armrest, his snores like the sound of thunder. I'd take off his slippers and place a blanket over him. I'd clear up the dribbles of sick that ran down his chin with a dirty tea towel. And I'd put the empty cans in a bin bag, then take that bin bag to the outside bin, as if to hide the evidence.

Then there was the day he hung himself in the garage and I returned home from school to find his limp, empty body.

To this day, I can't decide whether he was doing me a favour by ending his life. Whether he thought he was saving me from abuse as he robbed me of a father.

I bow my head. Close my eyes. Think a few words of solace and guilt, then immediately regret thinking them. It is hard to produce words for my father that are either kind or unkind, as both seem to betray who he was.

I feel a presence behind me. A soothing one. Her perfume floats across the wind. She reaches my side and places a hand in mine. I don't need to turn around to know that she's there.

"I was wondering if you would come," I say.

"Of course I am here," April tells me. "I never forget this day."

I consider telling her how I feel. Sadness over Dad's death; love for her I bury deep down; despair at the path that life has forced me on.

As it is, I say nothing. And she says nothing. And all that we should say passes between us without a single word.

It's the best way to say it.

She waits until I'm ready. She looks at the grave and holds her body close to mine, possibly for warmth, possibly for something else.

After a while, I nod at Dad. I don't tell him I love him—we were never that kind of father and son; the kind that let each other know how they feel; the kind that acknowledged the simple parts of our complicated relationship. Such words never felt appropriate. Instead, a manly gesture would suit his temperament, despite how little it suits mine.

We turn and wander across the graveyard until we reach a bench. We sit down and she lets go of my hand so she can wrap her arms around her body. She'd rather provide her own warmth.

"The Church hasn't sanctioned an exorcism on Billy Tate," she tells me.

I scoff. I was expecting as much.

"Not officially, anyway," she adds.

"Not officially?"

"They know he's possessed—they trust you that much."

"That's kind of them." I shake my head and look away. The wind carries a single leaf across the grass. I watch it as it dances.

"They are concerned about image."

"What image?"

"A double murderer in prison. It's a high-profile case. Things will get out. It will draw too much attention."

"And what about doing the right thing?"

"You know how it is, Mo."

I nod. I do know how it is. And it reminds me exactly why I left.

"That's why we can't get involved," she says. By *we* she means her and the rest of the Sensitives; the ones who still play by the Churches' rules. The ones who care more about secrecy than the damnation of a man's eternal soul. "But you can."

"I can?"

"They have agreed to instruct the prison to give you the time alone you need with him. We need to know which demon is possessing him."

"And it's the guy who's off the books that does this. The one that the Church can publicly condemn if anyone finds out."

"I'm afraid so."

"And if I say no?"

She smiles that smile; it kills me every time. "They are still paying you, Mo. Even if it's not officially."

"So I'm still their pawn?"

"Come on—we both know that you would help this man regardless of what the Church says. They are only helping because they are afraid of what you might do if they don't have any involvement whatsoever."

"Ah, I see. They can't stop the fire, so they may as well pour gasoline on it and look away."

"Something like that." She chuckles. "That was quite the metaphor—have you been reading or something?"

I chuckle too. I meet her eyes. Those eyes. What I'd give to see my love mirrored in those eyes.

"Find out who the demon is," she says.

"I tried—I touched his hand, but I couldn't see its true form. That's never happened to me before."

"But you're still sure there's something inside of him?"

"I have no doubt."

"Then it's even more important that we find out what we're dealing with."

I nod. She always knows the right thing to say. It's an ability I've always envied.

"And I assume you can't be involved?"

"Not officially, no."

"Ain't that a bitch."

A silence rests between us. It's not awkward—our silences rarely are—but it's not an easy silence.

She reaches across and squeezes my hand. Then she retracts her hand and places it in her pocket as she stands.

I stand too. Close enough to touch her but far enough away that it doesn't feel right to do so.

Neither of us turns to go.

She opens her mouth to speak, but doesn't. Yet again, the unsaid prevails, and our words are not enough.

She opens her arms and places them around me. I hug her back. It is both intoxicating and excruciating. I smell her hair. She pulls away.

"Take care of yourself," she says.

I nod.

She turns. Leaves. It doesn't take long until she's lost in the darkness, and I'm just a man alone amongst a bunch of graves.

Nine

It's early when I wake up.

Not that I can check the time on my phone—the moment I try to turn on the screen, I realise the battery is dead. But I can tell from the low sun rising over the field I've slept in that the day is only just beginning.

It was a chilly night, but I have a warm sleeping bag. Much as I have done many other nights, I found a field in the middle of nowhere, searched for the biggest tree, and laid under it, staring at the stars. At some point I fell asleep, though I struggle to pinpoint when. And now, as I wake naturally, I enjoy the morning hue, and revel in the feeling of serenity one can only find in nature.

So many people refuse to live like this, constraining themselves in marriage and mortgages. For me, this is the only way I can live. Wandering Earth in the way most won't approve of. Riding up and down the country on my motorbike and waking up somewhere new each night.

No one ever bothers me. The occasional fox might make a sound. An owl might hoot. The wind might pick up speed.

But here, in the middle of the field, I am peaceful. I feel truly free, and I pity those who pity me for it.

But I am also smelly, and I need a shower.

I take myself out of my sleeping bag and retrieve a bottle of water from the back of my motorbike. I drink most of it down in one. Then I pack away my sleeping bag and mount my metal steed. I kick away the stand, rev the engine, and find my way to the closest road.

I follow the signs to the nearest motorway, then stop at the nearest service station. There are only a few cars. Most people inside are men in suits having their breakfast. A clock hangs on the wall above the newsagents, and I notice it's just gone seven. I buy myself a bacon sandwich, eat it alone, then lock myself in the shower.

I've grown used to service station showers. I know to wait to check the water doesn't come out freezing or scalding; I've learnt not to use any shower gel that someone might have left as it may have been there for a long time; mostly, I've learnt that no one bothers me. People rarely use these showers.

Then again, who would use them but the homeless?

People have showers at home. Or in their caravans. Or in their hotels. Or at their campsite. I can't imagine anyone other than lorry drivers or nomads would ever need to make use of them.

So I take my time, ignoring the occasional conversations that move loudly past the door: blokes on business calls, kids complaining about being up so early, friends arguing over something or other. Conflict passes the door over and over, and each time, I am grateful that their life is not mine.

I finish. Dry my hair. Dry my body. Put on a fresh pair of underwear, along with a clean t-shirt, trousers, and socks. I emerge from the shower room into a busier service station. It's rush hour now, and everyone walks quicker, striding from one target destination to another. I walk between them until I reach a free table by a charger where I plug in my phone.

As soon as it turns on, the message alert pings for my attention. It's Olivia.

Prison have agreed to 3pm
They say it only happens if you're there
Don't know how you do it but you did

I can't read the tone of that last message.

That's the problem with texts—they are often so impersonal, and it's hard to read the subtext of what they have written. Either it's:

Impressed—*Oh wow, I really don't know how you did it, you're amazing.*

Resentful—*Of course it would have to be you who did it, you absolute dick.*

Horny—*Don't know how you did it, but you did and now I can't help picturing you naked.*

I chuckle to myself. I'm pretty sure it's not the last one.

Besides, it's not me who did it, it was the Church. If there is anyone she should be impressed/resentful/horny toward, it's them, and their ability to discreetly tamper with our everyday lives in a way that goes unnoticed by almost every person. Each commuter charging through this service station, hurriedly getting their coffee-to-go or having a quick pee, hasn't a clue. I wonder how they would react if they knew demons were real.

If it was me, I'd be sceptical. Demons still seem like a farfetched idea to me, and I fight the fuckers.

I text back.

. . .

Brill
Meet you at the uni before?

A few minutes pass. My attention drifts from the large queue for coffee, to the hurried workers making a dozen cappuccinos at once, to the grumpy faces that show little empathy for the difficulty it takes to provide them with such speed of service.

Another text message arrives.

Coffee first?

I smile.

She wants a coffee first?

Jeeze. I have absolutely no idea what tone that message was sent in.

Ten

She chooses a small independent coffee shop local to the university. It looks like a classy establishment, with bookcases in the corner and literary quotes on the wall, and I think I'm going to like it here—then it ends up full of rowdy students. They are at an age where they can shrug off a hangover and be as loud as they wish the next day, and it makes me resent them a little.

Olivia chooses a table in the corner, out of the way, the opposite side of the coffee shop to the doors and the windows; one cloaked in shadow, lit by only a single lamp, where we can be undisturbed.

I sit opposite her with a black coffee and she makes idle conversation, but I can tell she wants to ask me something. She keeps leaning forward, her hand resting permanently on the side of her skinny cappuccino, never touching the toasted teacake that the barista delivers.

She makes statements such as:

"It is feeling awfully cold at the moment."

"I don't think there's ever a day when I'm not tired."

"Yep, coffee, that's my fuel."

Until I cut in and say, "I'm not one for pointless small talk. Why don't you tell me what it is you really want to know?"

Now she leans forward. As if I have given her permission to finally talk about something that matters. Something important.

"I want to know more about who you are," she says. Her voice is hushed and discreet, but her eyes are glowing.

"Who I am?"

"Yes. A Sensitive. I'm fascinated by what that even is."

I smile and watch the steam rise from my beverage. Here, I thought this was an olive branch, a way to undo the hostility she's held toward me. But it's not. It's academic fascination. Curiosity. Irritation that I can do what she can't.

"Where would you like me to start?" I ask, returning my reluctant gaze to her eager eyes.

"How did you manage to get us alone with Billy Tate? There's no way the prison would agree to that." "The Church holds more authority than the prison. It keeps the truth secret and the public safe, and it does it by infiltrating and controlling almost everything."

"The Church controls almost everything?"

I nod.

"How do you know this?"

"Because, as a Sensitive, I used to be employed by them."

"Used to?"

"Let's just say we disagreed about the importance of maintaining their image over doing what's right."

"And Sensitives, how did they come about? Have there always been Sensitives?"

"No."

"Then where did they come from?"

I shift in my seat. Look around. People are engrossed in their conversations, and there's no one that can overhear; not that they'd believe what I'm about to say if not.

"Heaven conceived Jesus Christ, yes?"

"That's what we're led to believe."

"So what do you think it would look like if a person was conceived by Hell?"

"Oh, wow. I don't know. They would be the antichrist, I guess?"

I nod. "You're spot on."

"Are you telling me that's actually happened? How are we all safe?"

"That's a good question. People often thought that the turn of the millennium would mean the return of Christ, but it was The Devil that owned the year 2000. It's what led to the Edward King war."

"The what?"

"Hell conceived a man called Eddie, though this remained unknown to him until his friend and mentor, Derek Lansdale, discovered it."

"Derek Lansdale? I recognise that name."

"I've been told he was a great man."

"Was?"

"He died before my time."

I pause to sip my coffee. Impatient, Olivia prompts me to continue.

"Well, what happened?"

"The Hell that lived inside of Eddie grew stronger. Eventually, it took Eddie over, and he manifested into his true form; he became the Heir of Hell, and he almost brought this world to an end. Fortunately, there was still a piece of the human inside of him, and the woman he loved more than anyone—his best friend—was able to bring that out in him. He destroyed himself to save the world."

"Wow..."

Her jaw hangs low. I expected scepticism, but I can see she

believes me completely—just as I can see that she cannot choose which of her dozens of questions to ask first.

"Surely we would all know about this? If demons are battling us on earth, then—"

"The Church is very good at covering it up."

"And what has this got to do with the Sensitives?"

I take another sip of my coffee. I enjoy keeping her in suspense.

"The Sensitives were a response to what Hell did. There was an agreement after Christ that Heaven would conceive no more humans, so long as Hell didn't—Hell betrayed this agreement. In response, Heaven conceived many, many people, all of whom were born with a gift—the ability to sense and control the supernatural. We now work in secret to ensure that The Devil never achieves what he wants most—to allow demons to walk this earth, and to unleash Hell. Which, they almost did."

"They almost did?"

"Yes. In another battle, a few years ago. Until a man sacrificed himself to save the world. And the Church released a virus into the world to ensure that we were distracted, and that we would never realise what the true cause of all the suffering was."

"Covid?"

I nod. Finish my coffee.

She says nothing. Her food and drink remain untouched. She stares at me, her mouth dropped.

"And how am I meant to believe all this?" she asks.

I laugh. I can't help it. It isn't my job to convince her of anything.

"You can believe whatever the hell you want," I say. "I couldn't give a shit."

She frowns. "Why are you so hostile?"

"Me? Hostile?"

"Yes. Very."

"If you'd met my father, you'd understand."

"Your father is an angry man?"

"*Was* an angry man. It was the anniversary of his death yesterday."

"Oh, I'm sorry."

"I'm not."

"If it helps, I didn't even know my father."

"It doesn't help."

I stand. We're going to be early if we leave now, but I've had enough of this conversation.

She finishes her coffee. Takes a bite of her teacake and leaves the rest. Stands. Joins me, and walks out next to me, and as she does, her hand brushes against mine.

Our skin meets.

And I fall to my knees.

Something I cannot see or sense hits my skull, like a boulder, something hard, something prompted by the gentle nudge of her flesh, and I am dazed, and I cannot tell where I am.

Her hand is on my back. Her voice is in my ear, asking if I'm okay. But it's like she's shouting in another room. I can't hear a word. My head is full of something else.

Flames.

Fury.

Vengeance.

Wrath.

Merciless slaughter.

Pain shoots up and down my side; rage penetrates my skull; flames surround me; hot; licking me; reaching for me; grabbing me; radiating off her like a rancid stench.

When it ends, I realise people are looking at me. Only Olivia has come to my aid, but people have stopped eating, stopping sipping their coffees to stare, to marvel at this strange man having an episode in the coffee shop entrance.

"Are you okay?"

I look up at her.

She looks down at me.

And I don't know what that was. What I felt. What I saw. But it was something from inside of her; something she does not know exists.

"Mo? Are you okay?"

"I – I'm fine."

She reaches out a hand, but I don't take it. I don't want to feel like that again, like the world is lost, like everything's hopeless, like I'm angry at everyone. I use a nearby table instead to steady myself as I stand.

"What is it?"

I realise I'm staring at her. It must be disconcerting to watch me gaping at her with such morbid intrigue. I cannot help it. There is something behind her eyes. I try to see what it is, but I don't try too hard—I'm not sure I want to know.

There is something inside of this woman, and she has no idea.

It is not a demon. I know that.

Aside from that, I have no idea what just happened.

It's never happened before.

"Do you need to go to the hospital?"

"No. I'll be fine. Let's just go."

She puts a hand on my back. I flinch.

"I'm fine," I say, batting her arm away, and I walk toward the exit, hobbling at first, irritated by the eyes that watch me leave.

She keeps glancing at me as we get in her car.

I keep my eyes away from hers and try to pretend that what just happened was nothing.

Eleven

We go through the regular rigmarole of entering the prison—surrendering our keys, our phones, and letting them search my small, brown leather bag—then we are led to a room by the prison warden, who pauses outside of it.

He turns to us. Looks us up and down. Clearly aggrieved by the intrusion—by the audacity of someone overriding his authority in the prison. He looks like a man incapable of smiling, who gets off on telling others what to do. Allowing us this liberty must be excruciating for him.

"Let me make something clear before you go in," he says, looking down his nose at me, then at Olivia. "This is *my* prison. It adheres to *my* rules. And I do not take kindly to *my* prisoners being upset in a way that makes life hard for *my* prison officers."

I step toward him, enter his personal space, and grin. "I don't think you have much of a say in it, do you?"

I step past him and open the door to the room that Billy occupies. Olivia follows and shuts the door behind her. Boy, that felt good.

Billy sits in the centre of the room in what must be an older, unused part of the prison. I imagine this was once a shower room, with tiles that are cracked and rotten, stained with colours formed by age. There are no windows, no other doors, and no sounds of people nearby. The only sound is silence, underscored by an occasional distant drip, the source of which I cannot determine.

Billy himself—or, at least, whatever is inside of him—sits serenely. He is calm, a small smile hidden in the darkness of his features, his hands on his lap. He wears nothing but torn shorts. He must have refused to get dressed, and the warden did not want to upset the instructions of those in authority that demanded Billy be here at a certain time.

"Hello, Billy," I say, carrying my bag to the wall, where I place it on the floor. I take out the items that prison officers scowled or chuckled at as they checked for smuggled contraband. Rosary beads. A bible. Holy water. I leave them spread out on the floor and collect my wooden crucifix, which I keep tight in my grip.

Olivia stands back. Watches. Doesn't interfere. She's done dozens of exorcisms, but this might just be the first actual demon she's going to witness.

I stand a few steps away from Billy. Legs apart. Shoulders back. Strong, confident posture. Despite its sinister smirk, I refuse to portray anything but confidence toward a demon that has so far disguised its identity from me.

This session is all about finding out who the demon is, nothing else. Once I have its name, I have the power, and I remind myself to keep focussed on my mission.

"Billy, if you are in there, then please listen."

Billy straightens his back, his bones cracking as he does. He lifts his chest and I notice how thin he is. Bones press against his skin like turkey bound in string. His spindly legs lack almost any muscle. The demon probably isn't letting him eat.

"I need your help," I say. "I know this is tough, but I am here to help you. For now, I need you to stop fighting whatever's in you. I need to speak to it, and it only. I know it's hard, but please do that for me."

A low, grave chuckle, each *ha* elongated, reverberates around the room. Billy is already gone.

"And now I speak to the *thing* that's inside of you, whatever you are. I demand you tell me why you torment this servant of God."

It doesn't answer.

"I demand you to–"

It shushes me. A loud, long shush. It takes me by surprise. Then it tilts its head and twists its neck, creating more audible cracks of Billy's bones, and rests its gaze on Olivia.

"*You came back...*" it says.

Olivia glances at me. She's confused. So am I.

"Demon, I command you to tell me your name."

It ignores me. Keeps its focus on her.

"*I knew you would...*"

I raise my crucifix and aim it at the demon. "Tell me your name."

"*We have a whole lot of history...*"

"I've only met you once," Olivia says, and I scowl at her for responding to it.

The demon laughs.

"*You have no idea, do you...*"

I step forward, place the crucifix against its head. A little smoke rises. It relishes the pain like a sunbather soaking up rays of sun.

"In the name of our Lord, tell me your name."

It ignores the burning and keeps its eyes on Olivia.

"*It's you... After all this time, it's you...*"

I keep the crucifix against its head and place my hand around Billy's bicep.

Normally, a simple touch would allow me to see this demon, but it's concealing its identity; it's hiding it from me, and I don't know how. It's never happened before. I press the crucifix harder against its head, expecting to see what has latched onto Billy's soul, but still I see nothing.

Why can I not see this demon's true form?

"Come here..."

I close my eyes. Focus. Concentrate. Try to see the horns. The head. The body. Which animal it rides. Anything to give me a hint.

All I see is fire. Rage. Burning.

Much like I saw in Olivia.

I open my eyes. Turn toward her.

She is walking forward. Her eyes wide. Seemingly unable to stop herself.

"Olivia, stay back!"

But she couldn't if she wanted to. The demon has enthralled her. It beckons her, and she obeys.

"Olivia, I said stay back!"

The demon raises Billy's arm.

I press the crucifix against his face, and I shout, I command, "Stop, demon! I command you, in the name of God, to stop!"

But I have no effect on it whatsoever.

This has never happened to me before.

Billy's hand opens, and Olivia's arm stretches toward it, and their fingers interlock.

As soon as they touch, Olivia falls to her knees, her skin attaches to his, and she is screaming, screaming, screaming.

I drop the crucifix and put my arms around Olivia. I try to pull her away, dragging her, pushing her—but she will not move.

Billy joins in the screams, only there is more than one voice in his, and Olivia keeps bellowing, looking upwards, her pupils dilating until they are fully black.

"Olivia!"

A crescendo of anguish drowns out my voice.

Screaming.

Roaring.

Screeching.

I grab their hands, try to pull them apart, try to remove the fingers from their grip on each other, but something stops me, something makes it too strong.

Billy's body shakes. Seizes. Guttural screams become high-pitched, then low again, going up and down, creating sounds no human could feasibly produce.

My focus remains on Olivia.

As much as Billy's hollers are cocky and manic, full of glee, hers are a complete contrast, consisting of nothing but agony; she's hurting, she's in pain, and she needs to be released.

I hold my arm back and aim my fist at their interlocked hands, but it does not break them apart.

I notice the crucifix on the floor. I pick it up. Press it against their hands. Smoke rises. I press the crucifix down harder with one hand and pull with my other, and eventually I am able to break them apart.

Olivia scarpers backwards, rushing away, crawling, until she reaches the corner of the room and stares at the thing that had compelled her.

The thing within Billy smirks in her direction.

"Come on," I say, quickly packing my equipment into my bag and pulling Olivia to her feet.

"*Be seeing you...*" it says as we flee the room.

She keeps staring at it until we're gone.

Twelve

I ignore the prison warden's rants about disturbing their patient and upsetting his prison and all the other self-aggrandized nonsense he comes out with. I just try to get Olivia out of there, and to the car, and to do so as quickly as I can.

When we finally reach the car, she is still shaken up, so I take the keys and unlock it, and we both get in.

Then I sit. Still. Silent.

She sits still just the same, except that while I stare at her, she stares adamantly ahead. Barely blinking. Not moving.

I give her a few minutes. The demon showed her something, and I must let her digest whatever it was—but I also know that I'm going to have to ask some hard questions. I need to know what passed between them; it is the only way for me to understand what this thing is.

Eventually, I go to speak, but she raises a hand to stop me. Then she opens it and says, "Keys."

I place the keys in her hand.

She turns the ignition. Puts her seatbelt on. Puts the car into gear. Every movement is jilted, robotic, cold. She reverses out of the car parking space, pulls the car onto the road, and drives under the speed limit.

I wait for the right time to talk. It doesn't arrive. I glance at her a few times, go to speak, but there is something in her expression, a vague but clear trauma, and it reminds me how little practice I have in speaking to people.

Demons, fine. I can argue with them all day. I can fight them all night, too. But people...

Demons want one thing—to remove the soul of the body they occupy, and to take that body for themselves. I know where I stand with them. I know how to perform an exorcism, and I know the solution.

But people...

People always come with so many layers. So many complexities. They are rarely categorised easily into good and evil. You must find the right way to get the best out of someone.

And right now, I do not know what that is.

After a long drive, she pulls up at the university.

I don't get out. Neither does she.

We just sit. Wait. For what, I'm not sure—for me to speak, maybe?

I can never tell.

"I know this is tough," I say, opening my mouth and seeing what comes out. "But I need to know what passed between you. I need to know, so I can help Billy, and you."

She bows her head.

"I need to know, Olivia."

She shakes her head.

"I need to-"

"I don't get it. Am I a Sensitive?"

I consider this. I don't want to shoot her down, but a Sensitive knows when they've found someone like them, and I do not feel it in her.

"No," I tell her. "You're not."

"Then how did I... How did that thing... How did it do that to me?"

"I... I don't know, Olivia. That's why I need your help to figure it out."

She shakes her head again, this time with more vigour.

"No, I just, I—no..."

I go to ask her another question but decide not to push it. Maybe she needs time. Not that we have time, but pushing her will not help. Perhaps giving her space is the best long-term solution.

"Fine," I tell her, and go to get out of the car.

She grabs my arm. I pause, halfway out the door, and turn to her.

She finally meets my eyes.

"I know I'm not a Sensitive, but there's something... familiar. Something I felt in him."

I nod. Smile. Reassure her.

"We'll figure it out. I'll meet you tomorrow."

She doesn't respond.

I step out of the car and walk toward my motorbike. By the time I look back, she's driven away.

Thirteen

Static plays on the radio. Olivia doesn't notice. She's too entranced by empty thoughts. Too engrossed in the absence inside of her mind. She is full of questions, but not a single one presents itself; she is too full of confusion to engage in rigorous contemplation.

She takes a while to realise that she's home. That she arrived a while ago. That she's been sitting in the driveway, staring at the steering wheel, with not a flinch in her body.

She shakes her head. Shuffles her body. Tries to break herself out of this funk.

She grabs her bag and steps out of her car. The bushes and flowers and clean lawn are as she left them. A large, warm house awaits, with only her possessions inside. How she wishes she had someone she loved inside, waiting for her with a glass of wine and a home-cooked meal. As it is, she has cheap prosecco in the fridge and a cheap lasagne to put in the microwave.

She steps inside, met with wooden floors and bare wooden wall panels and wooden furniture. She chose this décor, and she suddenly hates it. Everything is so wooden, so brown, so dull. She wants to change all of it.

She dumps her bag on the table. Opens the fridge. Puts the lasagne in the microwave. Sets the timer. Leans against the counter, folds her arms, and ruminates.

Now the questions start coming.

What happened to Billy?

Was that really what a demon is capable of?

And what the hell did it mean by *It's you*?

After all this time...

You have no idea...

Be seeing you...

What time? What does she not know? And why will it be seeing her?

The microwave pings, but she doesn't notice; she's too busy charging into the living room and opening her laptop. An empty wine glass and an open pad sit beside it, left over from an evening of reading her students' dissertations. She thinks back to the person who sat in this chair yesterday, contentedly noting down feedback, and she finds herself envying her. That woman thought she knew so much, but it turns out she barely knew anything at all.

She turns on the laptop. Loads the internet. And she searches.

Edward King.

She scans the results. Nothing. Not a single word. Nothing to verify that a word of Mo's stories are true.

But then again, if this information was clouded in secrecy as he claimed, there wouldn't be, would there?

Perhaps secrecy was a convenient explanation. A good excuse for why she couldn't find any evidence. After all, a war between Heaven and Hell taking place on Earth then being covered up by the Church seems a farfetched concept.

But isn't this what she's studied for?

She's researched demons. Believed in them. Fought them —falsely, according to Mo. She's sought answers like this her whole life. Now the answers have been given to her, and she doesn't want to believe them?

She thinks of what else Mo mentioned. Another name comes to mind. Derek Lansdale.

She searches.

This time there are results, though none that clarify any of what Mo has told her. The pages Google suggests confirm that Derek Lansdale was a leading researcher in the studies of the paranormal. And, what's more, he worked at the university where she works. In fact, he was part of the department a few decades ago. Is that why she recognised his name?

But why would she not have read any of his research?

They have a policy of keeping journals published by their academics. All studies and research are documented and kept for future learning. If she's part of the same department, why has his name been kept from her, and why has she never read any of his journals?

Unless the journals have been kept secret...

She stands. Suddenly. Not intending to, but she does.

She must know.

She must find out if his journals are somewhere. She must see if this is true.

Mostly, she must find out who she is. Why the thing inside Billy claimed to recognise her. Why Mo is so unnerved by her.

And the answers must be at the university.

Somewhere.

She grabs her keys and returns to the car. She backs down the driveway, turns onto the road, and drives as quickly as the speed limits will allow.

Fourteen

I sit alone in the park, breaking off pieces of the last French stick the supermarket had to offer and placing them in my mouth. It tastes dry, but my empty stomach welcomes it nonetheless. I did consider going to a fast-food restaurant or a late-night cafe, but I crave solace, and a place such as this rarely forces company on me at night. Darkness has forced happy mothers and eager children away, replaced by a silence that is only broken by the occasional shouts of drunks, or the intimidating presence of passing teenagers with their hoods up.

Sometimes they look at me. As if trying to conjure fear. Like they need me to turn away and avoid eye contact to make them feel valuable. But they don't scare me. They do not know what I've seen.

Once you've looked into the eyes of Hell, you find that the angry strut of rowdy youths rarely bothers you.

It doesn't take long until I barely acknowledge the rare presence of passers-by. I am so entrenched by my tumultuous thoughts that I don't notice the cold, either. There are too many conundrums, too many questions, too few answers, and I hate not knowing.

Olivia is not a Sensitive.

I know that for certain.

But she also isn't... I don't know... Right...

And Billy.

There isn't a demon inside of him.

But there's some*thing* inside of him.

But if it's not a demon, then what?

It's evil, that's for certain. It's deranged, feeding off his soul, desperate for carnage, for the end of days, for...

The end of days?

That's a huge target for one lowly demon to aim for.

It would take many demons, and sustained aggressive intervention from Hell, to launch an attack that might end our way of life. It's happened twice, and they've been thwarted, and it's taken time—but one little demon could not think it can create such a devastating impact alone.

But is it a demon?

What is it, if not a demon?

What else has Hell spewed up?

I lean my head back. Close my eyes. Linger on the problem, focus on the question, obsess over the peculiarities, and–

Oh, Lord.

I stand. Tense. Hairs on my arm stick on end. My muscles tense. I feel colder. Suddenly, so much colder.

I can't stay still. I rush from one side of the path to the other.

It can't be... It can't...

But my immediate thought brings with it the feeling of truth, and I know that denial will only delay intervention.

Who should I call?

Who should I focus on first?

Tell April? Get to Billy? Help Olivia?

So many thoughts, so many questions, so many terrifying possibilities.

But I know.
I know what it is.
I know what's inside of Billy.
And it's far, far worse than I could have imagined.

Billy Speaks

I know you're not me.

    I know.

    I can tell.

    I don't know how, but I can.

    And you need to stop.

    I don't understand, but you need to stop.

    I'm not crazy.

    Not insane.

    Not like they say I am.

    I am not a murderer. Not a man who would hurt his family.

    You did it.

    YOU did it.

    You and only you.

    Calm down, Billy, you're going to hurt yourself.

    Hurt?

    Myself?

    Leave me alone.

    Whatever you are, leave me alone.

I don't want you here. You're not welcome in my body. Just leave.

How could I do that, Billy?

How could I ever leave?

How could I part us now?

Stop it.

Stop this façade, this pretending, this acting like you care about me, like this is love and not possession, like this is caring and not ownership, stop it, just stop it.

I thought I told you to calm down.

GO TO HELL.

Oh, don't you worry, we'll be there soon...

I drop my head. Sniff. Refuse to cry. If other prisoners hear me from their cells, if other inmates sense my weakness, if these murderers perceive my vulnerability, then they will use it.

God, I hate this.

I can't show weakness despite being weak.

I can't show innocence despite being innocent.

And I can't show sanity when there is an incessant voice inside of me.

Sometimes it vibrates my bones. Sometimes it's deep, like a bass line that underscores a heavy metal song, it shakes my lungs, trembles my muscles. Then it's high-pitched, moments of madness, moments of screeching, pounding against the constraints of my skull.

Then sometimes—and these are the moments I hate the most—it sounds exactly like me.

Like it isn't separate from me. Like it isn't different. Like it isn't something else entirely.

I'm not crazy. But I sound crazy. There is something inside of me, and if I say it, I sound mad.

But there's definitely something.

Something that once belonged to someone else.

Belong?

Stop it, Billy.
I don't belong to anyone.
You're right. There is nowhere you belong.
I'm growing tired of you.
Then why don't you leave?
Yeah, if you're growing tired, then go.
Let me be at peace.
Let me serve out a life sentence without the torture coming from inside as well as out.
Don't worry, Billy.
Don't worry.
You won't have to serve a life sentence.
What, you're going to get us out of here?
Yes, I am—but that's not what I mean.
Please, just go…
I meant that it won't be long now.
Won't be long until you're gone.
Somewhere distant.
Somewhere far away.
Leaving your vessel.
Leaving it for me.
This damaged body, free for me to grow.
You are only here so long as I need you, so long as your breathing is required for my survival.
The second I'm strong enough.
The second it happens.
I will snatch away your soul and eat it and shit it out so your eternal being can be eaten by flies.
What happened to love? To caring? To us being together?
Grow up, Billy.
There's no need to pretend anymore.
I don't need you to accept me for my survival.
I don't want to kill any more people.
It won't be you.

My body isn't a weapon you can aim—it's mine.

You have no right to it.

No right? This body is the one I was born into—it has been mine ever since I was created!

And this Earth you walk upon has been ours since it was created.

We roamed; we were here; we had it first; you want to talk about what belongs to whom; then we deserve your home; we deserve it all.

Never speak to me about fairness.

Fuck you.

A shooting pain fires up my inside. It feels like a fist squeezing my heart, like knives piercing my lungs, like teeth biting my intestines.

It's agony.

Uncontrollable, unavoidable agony.

And it has me on the floor. Rolling. Writhing. I don't realise I'm screaming until inmates from adjacent cells scream with me, hooting and hollering. Screws shout to shut up. They don't. I don't. I can't.

I punch my mattress. Kick the wall. Pound my head against the floor.

I want to be knocked out.

I want to be unconscious.

Anything so I won't have to endure this.

Then it releases me.

And I lie here. Panting. Listening to the shouts from other inmates gradually die down. Feeling the aftermath of an intense pain, like the small patter of rain that follows a storm.

Once it subsides, once it all dies down, once the pain turns to numbness, I hear it. Chuckling. At the back of my mind. Mocking me with its long, drawn-out laughter.

Why?

Why me?

Why now?
Convenience. Ease. Susceptibility.
Please, just end this.
The only way I can end this is if you give in.
If you accept me.
If you sit back and allow me to take over.
Fine.
Fine, do it.
Whatever.
Whatever it takes to make it end.
Just do it.
I knew you'd come around.
I close my eyes and sink back.
I see darkness, and it's quickly overtaken by flames.
I'm not in here anymore.
I have faded away.
I'm sorry for whatever happens next.

BEFORE

Fifteen

A frustrating drive home always follows a long day at work. It's forty minutes from work to home, and whilst the commute at first appears annoying, it turns out to be exactly what Billy needs. He rants at the steering wheel, sings to loud music, and occasionally bemoans other drivers, meaning that, by the time he's almost home, the anger is all but gone. Which is important, considering it's his anniversary. Ten wonderful years with Jennifer to be celebrated by a wonderful meal out. They will drop Tilly off at her grandparents, put on some fancy outfits, and go for a meal so posh it's taken the whole of the last year to save for it.

But first, Billy needs to pick up the most important ingredient of a successful anniversary—flowers. The most expensive ones in the supermarket. So he parks outside the supermarket closest to his home, enters the store, and purchases a beautiful bouquet of red and yellow roses.

Perfect.

With an eager stride, he returns to his car singing the tune of their favourite song.

He passes a couple pushing a trolley full of their weekly

shop back to their car. He smiles at a young man carrying an old lady's shopping to her car boot. And he notices a mother loading her shopping into her car with a young child on the trolley chair—perhaps six or seven—staring at him.

He smiles at the child. Nods.

The child does not reciprocate.

The mother isn't aware. She is busy loading her car and is not paying attention to her child. Her child who will not stop staring.

Slowly, Billy's smile fades. He feels irritated. He quells it. Children are not always aware of social norms by such an age. They do not know that you should not stare.

Billy forces another smile. One he hopes ends the problem.

The child just stares.

Still, just stares.

Gormless. Intent. Annoying.

"What?" Billy says as he unlocks his car.

The mother remains clueless.

Bloody parents. Too distracted to know what their kids are doing. Too busy to teach them not to be rude.

"Knock it off."

Billy's arms are shaking.

Why are his arms shaking?

Is this really making him so angry?

"I said knock it off!"

Something whispers into his ear. Something distant but close. Loud but silent. Sinister yet loving.

Find the girl find the girl find the girl.

What girl?

This is a boy that's staring at him.

"I said piss off!"

Finally, the mother looks.

But it's too late.

Billy is charging across the car park, fists curled, heart racing, lip shaking, rage bursting at his skin.

It's not his rage.

Billy doesn't have rage.

He has patience. Kindness. Understanding.

But he feels this rage much the same.

Find the girl find the girl find the girl.

What fucking girl?

"Stop looking at me, you little shit!"

Still, the kid stares.

Still, the kid persists.

Still, the kid, the little ingrate, the little worm, the ugly little shit—still he stares.

The mother tries to turn the kid away. She lifts him out of the trolley and tries to pull him toward her car.

The kid doesn't move. He's unresponsive. Empty. Pathetic.

"I said to stop staring at me, you disgusting little cunt!"

The mother pulls at her son's arm, tugs at it, drags at it. The boy is like a tree, roots beneath the ground, unyielding in the face of pressure.

"I'll fucking kill you!"

He reaches the child.

Reaches out for him.

Stretches for the kid's throat.

And a blackness descends.

When he opens his eyes, the kid is on the floor, gurgling, spluttering, desperate, coughing.

It takes a few seconds for Billy to realise why.

To realise that it's his hands on the kid's throat.

That it's him the mother is screaming at.

He stands. Quickly. Looks around. Bemused.

People are walking toward him. Big, beefy blokes approaching from across the car park, demanding to know what Billy thinks he's doing, responding to the mother's calls for help.

Billy doesn't know what to do. He wants to help, wants to make sure the kid is okay, but these blokes look angry, and he's never been in a fight in his life, he's scared, he doesn't know–

The kid coughs. He breathes. He's okay.

Billy sprints to his car. He leaves the flowers on the floor and crushes them with the front wheel as he spins his car around.

The blokes are shouting at him. Striding after his car. The woman is screaming for help.

They all want to hurt him.

He accelerates out of the car park, onto the road, and away.

Find the girl find the girl find the girl.

He does not know what that means.

NOW

Sixteen

There is a section of the library that hides behind the reception. A section where students don't go. A section that has a reputation for shame and secrecy. A section full of dusty books that no one ever finds useful.

Olivia intends to scour this section, to search every cabinet if she must. If the university is hiding secrets, it will surely be in the hidden pages of that room.

The library is silent. Despite being three in the morning, the rare student sits at a table with headphones on, pulling an all-nighter to meet the imminent deadline of an assignment. They are disinterested in her, and she can stride between aisles of books knowing that there is no one watching her.

She glances over her shoulder, slides across the empty reception desk, and approaches a large wooden door. The handle is loose, but it turns, and it creaks open into a vast room, full of shelves and cabinets with dusty, leather-bound books and envelopes of pages.

With no other logical starting point, she begins her quest on the shelf furthest to her right, intending to keep searching to her left until she finds something of interest.

She finds periodicals from scientific journals from the 1970s. Browned pages of diary entries from previous deans of the university. Newspapers from decades and decades ago. A vast amount of history contained within the room, but none of it is useful to her.

She searches the next shelves. Old medicine manuals with outdated advice. More old newspaper copies. Chronicles of years gone by.

She coughs from the dust. Wipes her hands on her blouse. Renews her determination to find what she's after and continues searching the shelves.

Half an hour goes by and all she has to show for it is a dry throat and dust in her eyes.

She finishes scanning another set of horizontal shelves and moves to a cabinet. She opens the first draw and searches the various titles. They appear to be journals from former lecturers. This is closer to what she's searching for, even if the lecturers are all discussing topics that have nothing to do with what she's after.

Pharmaceuticals. Psychoanalysis. Medieval history.

There is an abundance of knowledge here, and there are so many things to learn about, but none of them are relevant.

She moves to the next draw, dismisses many irrelevant subjects, then lowers herself to the last draw at the bottom of the cabinet. She flicks past unknown names and fascinating but useless topics, until finally, after a search that finds her deep into the far depths of the draw, yawning into the back of her sleeve and rubbing her eyes with her wrist, she finds it.

The Journals of Derek Lansdale.

She pulls them out. They appear to be copies. She wonders where the originals are. Then again, who cares—she has them. They are real. Mo was right.

At least, he was right that this man existed—she hasn't read the contents yet.

With care and enthusiasm, she carries them to the nearest table and spreads them out. Flicks through pages that have remained untouched for years, documentation of things that happened years ago. There are so many pages that it would take her too long to read all of them.

So she scans them, searching for The Edward King War.

Until she finds it in his last ever journal entry.

August 2003

It's almost as if it never happened.

I understand the need for secrecy. For silence. Just imagining the repercussions of what might have happened should we have lost is enough to terrify any regular adult or child. The world's population will never comprehend how close their species came to annihilation and eternal torment. I feel sick at the thought of what our reality almost became, and I feel a deep sadness that we are deceiving the human population so severely from a truth they would probably never accept.

But it's not the Edward King War I feel bad about hiding. It's not the concealment of a war more epic than any previously fought by mankind. It's not the truth of what exists in this world that I feel guilty for keeping within the realm of nightmares.

It is the heroics of Edward King that I feel for.

The legacy of my closest friend.

Eddie was a good man, and he showed that in the end. Despite the deaths caused by the thing inside of him, the thing that took over, it was the human element that won. Eddie proved that kindness can be the victor over evil, despite the vehemence and strength of the evil's onslaught.

Within hours of the war ending, the bodies had already been taken away, the blood had disappeared from the grass, and the buildings had been restored. There is no reminder that a brave, courageous man has conquered the greatest, purest evil one could ever encounter.

And that is why I must leave.

The dean begged me to stay. Despite the ridicule and mocking my department receives, he believes in my research, and he did not want to see me go. There are others, however, that can carry on with my work. This department will thrive under new leadership. For now, my place is away from this world.

One cannot witness such atrocities and then carry on as if the world is as it was.

Angel Gabrielle visited me. I wasn't expecting it, but the divine evidently felt it necessary to impart to me the knowledge of Heaven's intentions. A visit from an angel is a unique experience, and gave me a profound insight into the experience of the Virgin Mary, to whom I have a newfound respect. To endure the feeling of awe that accompanies a creature of pure nobility, and to persist in one's life as if the experience hasn't changed them, is to show grace that most mere mortals are rarely capable of.

She told me that Sensitives will be created. Those who are born from Heaven's light. And there will be others to guide them. I don't know what involvement I will have in this guidance. Not yet, anyway. We'll see.

For now, I bow my head for those we lost and the evil that dominated, and I raise a glass for the man I mourn.

The greatest man to ever live.

I do not know what the last moments of Eddie's earthly existence must have been like, but I imagine it would have involved ethical conundrums that would torment most of us. He would have had to decide between sacrifice and immortality; between his beloved sister and a new existence; between the knowledge of what he has done and what he can still do.

He was Hell's greatest weapon and the world's greatest saviour.

He was forged by the underworld, but saved by the man inside of him.

And who knows which will prevail next time—the good or the bad. A war of such evil requires incomprehensible divinity to beat it. I am not optimistic that the human in Eddie, who possessed the ability to fight what raged so intensely inside of him, would exist in many people. Should humankind encounter this threat again, I fear the strength that existed within Eddie will not exist in another, and that the honourable disposition needed to vanquish such a grave threat will not be powerful enough in the regular human.

But I hope that the world does not know an evil so strong again.

We would not survive another antichrist, so let us strive for a world where we do not face another one.

I fear for what would happen if such a threat arose again.

The risk would be too severe.

We would not endure another war.

Humankind would not have another Edward King.

And that is where it ends.

So much said, and so much to understand.

I sit back. Wipe sweat from my brow. I'm cold, but I'm also hot. I'm shivering, but I'm burning up.

I realise my phone is vibrating.

I take it out, and a call from Mo fails.

It's the seventeenth missed call from him.

He rings again, and I answer.

Seventeen

Finally, she answers.

"Olivia, where are you?"

"I'm at the university."

Her voice is loud in my headphones. I speed around another roundabout and change direction toward the university.

"We need to get to the prison now."

"Why?"

"I'll explain, just meet me at your car."

I hang up before she can object. I skid around a corner and speed across another street. I'm aware that my motorbike will be loud when I'm accelerating this quickly, and I'm shooting down residential areas late at night—but I'm also aware that the people I may be slightly inconveniencing by waking up, will be even more inconvenienced should they have to suffer a fiery apocalyptic death. So, really, they can deal with it.

"Hey Siri," I say, then add, "dial April."

It's the middle of the night, but even so, I know I can rely on April to pick up. She barely has time to adjust herself to waking up before I'm verbally unloading on her, telling her what I've realised, what I've discovered—telling her the precarious position we are in.

She is immediately concerned. She tells me we can't wait until morning. She will contact the Church and have them arrange for us to have immediate access to Billy. That we need to act quickly—he needs to be exorcised now.

She says that, if I'm right, it is of the utmost importance that we act now before things get any worse.

I pull up in the university car park minutes later. I see Olivia standing by her car in the empty car park, and I park beside her.

"We need to get to the prison," I tell her as I remove my helmet and climb into her passenger seat. Once she's climbed into the driver's seat, I add, "And quickly."

She reverses out of the space, directs us to the nearest road, and drives at the quickest acceptable speed.

I look out of the window and watch the world go by. The occasional street lamp; empty fields filled with darkness; frost on the leafless branches of large trees. It's strange how the beauty of nature can look so ominous in the dark.

"I found Derek Lansdale's journals."

I turn to her quickly. "Impossible, the Sensitives have them."

"The university has copies."

"For anyone to access?"

"No. They are in a cabinet in a large room of old documents. You wouldn't find them unless you were looking for them."

I breathe a sigh of relief. I'm not sure why. I'm not opposed to people knowing the truth.

"So did you read about The Edward King War?"

"Some. Did you ever know Eddie?"

"No."

"Did you ever know Derek?"

"No."

"So you know nothing?"

"I know what I was taught—and I know the importance of knowing it."

"What does that even mean?"

"It means that I know what we risk if we do not get to Billy in time."

Her eyes linger on me before returning to the road. She turns another corner down the country road. Not a single car passes us.

"So what demon is in Billy then?" she asks.

I go to answer, then hesitate.

"I assume you figured it out?"

"Yes. Yes, I did."

"So what demon is in him?"

I take a deep breath; she needs to know. "It's not a demon."

"Not a demon?"

"No. It's far worse."

"What?"

I run my hands over my face and through my hair. My lack of sleep becomes abruptly apparent. I fight away the fatigue.

"What do you know about The Edward King War?" I ask her.

"I know how it ends. I know Eddie defeated whatever was inside of him."

"It wasn't quite that simple."

"You're really not making any sense."

I take a deep breath, hold it, and let it go.

"The thing inside of Eddie was the heir to Hell. The Devil's messiah. It was evil in the purest form, more than any demon. Eddie was conceived by Hell, but it is impossible for him to be driven solely by Hell, as he has a human host. Hell was, for lack of a better way of putting it, Eddie's father—and his mother was human."

"So the evil could never take full control?"

"Precisely. The reason Eddie could defeat that evil is because the human part of him was still there. The evil could not remove it, meaning Eddie's soul could still fight. In the end, Eddie fought the evil inside of him."

"And he won?"

"Well, yes. And no."

"What do you mean?"

"Eddie defeated it, in the sense of he separated himself from it. Then *it* still exists. It must go somewhere. It wouldn't just disappear."

"So the antichrist, the heir of Hell, the purest evil ever—is... where, exactly?"

"We haven't known. A few years ago, the Sensitives were almost defeated, and more demons came onto the earth, and we all waited for *it* to appear, but *it* didn't. The sensitives fought The Devil, but this thing was never there."

"But surely it would be? If it still existed, I mean?"

"Unless it was a tactical decision. A strategy. A backup plan."

"A backup plan?"

"Just in case The Devil lost. If he went back to Hell, he'd have something else he could deploy. And it would come back to earth and try to finish what he started."

I'm out of breath. I'm talking too fast. I close my eyes, allow them to stay closed a little too long, then open them.

We pass a sign for the prison.

"I still don't get why this is relevant," she asks as she pulls into the car park.

"Because that *thing*—that backup plan—that purest evil that's ever existed, that could bring on the end of days — I believe it's back."

"It's back?"

"And it's close to gaining full strength. It just needs something else, though I'm not sure what. But it's almost taken over the body of its host."

"And you think the host is…"

"Billy, yes. I think it is inside Billy."

Eighteen

The screws are irritable, and I don't blame them. They don't like being overruled and they don't enjoy having to collect a prisoner at night and they don't like whatever nonsense we are doing to upset him and disturb the precarious balance of life within their prison walls.

But this is more important than them.

So we let them bring Billy in. The deathly stares they give us are no match for this creature's intense glare. There's an element of cockiness to it, of one-upmanship, of knowledge of the power it holds, whilst also a clear hatred for who we are and what we represent.

It will despise humans, and we are the worst kind of humans; those who play a part in the Heaven's triumph over evil. I bet it can't wait to rip us apart.

I annoy the prison officers further by asking them to help us remove all tables and chairs from the room. Once they have grudgingly done so, we stand in a room that is empty except for one chair; the one it sits in.

"Is Billy still in there?" I ask.

It doesn't reply. Just grins.

"Shouldn't we bind his wrists?" Olivia whispers in my ear.

I would normally agree, but not this time. "There's no point. It would do little to stop it."

It leans back. Waits. Like a judgemental examiner, eager to see what nonsense we come out with. Whatever it is, it will thwart it. It does not need to fear us. It will resist whatever attack we mount.

Unfortunately, that may lead to one solution.

Billy's death.

If we can't prevent the evil through exorcism, then this might be the only way—though it is not one I will entertain. The Church will sign off on his death should it be necessary, and they will do it without the hesitation or consideration a situation such as this requires—but I will not. He is a living person, and whatever is inside of him, whatever the risk to humanity, I can't take a life as easily as those who only think of the consequences to the world, and not to a suffering individual.

But there is something else I require. Something besides the removal of the entity.

I need information.

I need to know what it's after.

Why it's here.

And whether there is another war coming.

"Is Billy in there?" I repeat.

It raises its eyebrows and looks down at Billy's chest.

"*In here... Somewhere...*"

"Is he gone yet?"

"*He isn't gone... Not yet... But he is close...*"

"And his soul?"

"*His soul... It tastes like roast chicken and gravy...*"

I nod. I am unsure whether I can save him, but I refuse to allow this thought to fester—whilst I understand denial is the most useless of impulses, it is one I cannot help but allow.

The longer a demon remains in a body without being exorcised, the closer it gets to amalgamation incarnation—the process of the demon removing the soul from the body and taking the body for itself. From then on, there is none of the person left, and our aim is to avoid getting to that point by exorcising the demon first.

But this is no demon.

This is something far, far worse.

And it hasn't taken long for the greatest evil ever produced to take over the body.

But I refuse to consider the last resort. Not yet, at least. If ever.

So I open my bag. Take out my wooden cross. Take out the Rites of Exorcism that I know so well. And I turn to it, with a huge sigh, and wonder how futile this is going to be.

"So what's the plan?" I ask it. "Sit around in a prison cell, waiting for nothing? Not very formidable, is it... Not very cunning..."

"*Oh, we'll be out... Soon enough...*"

"Then why not now? What are you after?"

It doesn't reply. It doesn't even look at me.

"If you're so powerful, it won't matter if you tell me, will it?"

"*Oh, I don't know...*"

"What are you after?"

I realise why it isn't looking at me. It's because it's looking at Olivia.

Her worried stare switches from it, to me, to it, to me, and in her fear, I see her trying to deduce what its gaze means. I wish I could offer her an answer, but I can't.

Is it after her?

Why would it be after her?

"What are you after?"

It doesn't answer. Nor does it avert its gaze from Olivia,

and I feel the rage prompted by its lack of cooperation biting at my belly.

Enough. I've had enough.

It's time to begin.

"Haughty men have risen up against me," I begin, "and fierce men seek my life."

It laughs.

They always laugh.

"They set not God before their eyes."

I hold the crucifix out.

It sticks out Billy's tongue. Presses the end against the cross. Smoke rises and it burns, but it does not remove it—instead, it drags the tongue upwards, slowly, across the long side of the cross, like a child enjoying a lollipop, relishing the burn.

"In God's name, whose nature is ever merciful and forgiving, tell me what you are after."

It presses its tongue harder, and the smoke turns black, and I press the crucifix harder, and I press it against its face, and it grins and relishes the pain like it's a cold bucket of water on a summer's day.

"*Oh, yes! More! Yes, more! More!*"

"In the Holy Lord's name, almighty Father, everlasting God, our Lord Jesus Christ who once and for all consigned that fall and apostate tyrant to the flames of Hell—tell me what you are after!"

It opens its mouth wide, places its teeth on either side of the crucifix, and clamps down. Small sparks of flames like a lighter appear from its teeth, smoke growing thicker, rising higher, filling the room.

I know what it's doing.

I must not be deterred.

I will persist.

"Lord hasten our call for help and snatch from ruination

and from the clutches of evil this beast's intentions and command it—tell us what you are after!"

It bites down harder, its incisors pushing into the wood, sinking further, teeth wobbling, Billy's gums bleeding, slowly at first, then dripping down the crucifix, warming my knuckles.

"I command you, unclean spirit, with your minions attacking this servant of God—tell us what you are after!"

The wood of the crucifix cracks under the pressure of its jaw.

"Through Jesus, Son of Mary, Lord and saviour, I command you—tell us what you are after!"

Its teeth sink further through the crucifix until it splinters and separates and comes apart, and it keeps chomping, flames appearing in its jaw, fire raging out of its mouth, growing, licking at me, burning off pieces of God's symbol, and I stand back as it takes my crucifix and bites it apart until the pieces fall to Billy's lap as pieces of wood amongst ash.

It turns to Olivia.

Eyes narrowed.

Flames flickering low and dying out.

"Tell me what you're after!"

And finally, it answers—though it does not do so as a sign of my victory, but as a deliberate ploy to tease and torment—nevertheless, its voice protrudes from its lips, a voice different to Billy's, a contorted chaos of vocal chords, something unique, something inhuman, and it says, slowly and succinctly, "*Her.*"

I frown. Look at Olivia. Look back at it.

"*Once I am stronger... I have waited... And I am hours away from having the ability... The ability to take her...*"

"Her? Why her?"

"*I see you now... I know for sure... I have looked upon you and now I know for sure... I know what you are... And I know what I need..."*

"Tell me—why her?"

"Because she has me within her."

I step across the room, standing in front of Olivia, concealing her from it. She is defiant in the face of the entity, standing tall, but as my hands reach behind my back and close around her wrists, I can feel her shaking, I can feel her fear, and I understand why she feels such a fear despite her attempts to conquer and conceal it.

I understand, because I feel the same fear myself; this is not what I expected.

"She has got nothing of you in her," I say, refusing to let it taunt us. "She is human."

It shakes its head.

"She is his daughter."

His daughter?

Whose daughter?

We can't stay here. This isn't what I anticipated. This isn't safe.

"We're going," I decide. This is futile. This exorcism won't work.

I grab Olivia's wrist and drag her to the door, picking up my bag as I do.

Just as my hand brushes the door handle, Billy rises from the seat, sprints at us, barges into me and tries to reach past me, tries to grip its fingers around her arm. I hold it off, but it is strong. Too strong. I have no crucifix. I have no weapon.

"Back off!"

It does nothing.

Billy's limbs twist and turn, each pointing in obscure, wayward directions, its demented gaze fixed on Olivia.

It reaches for her.

I shouldn't have brought her here.

"I will have her..."

I open the door and call for the prison officers.

"I will have her..."

They run down the hallway and dive upon him.

"I will have Edward King's daughter..."

I freeze. Turn to her.

Her eyes are wide.

It can't be.

It's lying. It must be.

We need to go. We need to regather ourselves. To retreat and reflect.

We flee. Run to collect our possessions. Run to the car park. Run to the car. Run away.

She turns the ignition.

But I put my hand on the handbrake so she can't drive away.

"What are you doing?" she demands.

"I'm sorry," I say, placing my hand on the bare skin of her arm, hoping this knowledge will provide a vision of the truth. "I'm sorry, but I must know."

And as I place my skin against hers, I see it all; who she is; where she came from; why it's after her.

Clarity prevails.

I see the conception of Edward King's daughter.

I see everything...

———

Eddie wakes every night.

Except, it's not him.

It's him, but it's not.

And he despises the paradox.

He knows he's there. He's somewhere inside. But whatever it is growing inside of him, gaining strength, pushing against his chest—it takes control, and Eddie is but a bystander. A passenger. A guest.

He kicks homeless people; pushes drunks into bins; taunts women who walk alone; steals from people with their pockets unguarded; aims racist statements to the men who work in the kebab shop. He is vaguely aware of what he's doing, but by the time morning has passed its infancy, he no longer has any recollection of the evil deeds he commits; like a dream so intense you think you'll never forget it, but by the time you're out of bed, all recollection of it is gone, and just the feelings remain. He feels tired, sometimes even ill, with an ache in his muscles and a fatigue in his mind that a full night's sleep should have defeated. He is unaware of what the thing inside of him made him do, and he can continue with his day unperturbed.

On this particular night, on this particular occasion, he awakes, leaves the comfort of the makeshift bed he's created on his best friend's sofa, and walks aimlessly out of the house. His feet carry him forward in defiance of his confused mind, wandering with purpose but without direction. He ends up on the outskirts of town. Lurking in the shadows. Hiding on streets where there are no lampposts. Watching people pass unaware that someone witnesses their movements.

He sees a woman.

Miraculously beautiful, but also slightly bedraggled. She wears a purple dress that ends halfway down her thigh, revealing perfectly smooth legs that almost distract the casual observer from noticing the large wet patches beneath her armpits. Makeup that was impeccably applied at the beginning of the night is now faded or smudged. Long, blond locks, combed and forced into place with hairspray a few hours ago, now form clumps around her neck. She carries her high heels in her hand, preferring the discomfort of the tender soles of her feet treading on pavement over the pain of tight shoes with heels she struggles to balance in. A night on the town that seemed so full of opportunity at its beginning has seen her abandoned by friends and left to walk home alone.

The thing inside of Eddie is entranced, and he has no option but to follow her.

The thick of night conceals his movement. The moon is hidden by grey clouds and provides little clarity to figures in the dark. His footsteps are light, and he makes no noise.

The woman does not know he's there, but she senses something. She looks around, an instinctive glance over her shoulder. She clutches her keys in her jacket pocket. She walks a little quicker.

She resents her friends for leaving. They always provided her with such protection. On the dance floor of the nightclub, men would prowl, lurk, saunter—they would approach her friends as they danced together, minding their own business— they would try to press their grinding bodies up against her— her friends would immediately intervene, stepping in front of the lecherous men, dancing around her. They would enjoy their dances and protect each other from the predators.

Only, this night, they had all drunk too much, and one group of men were insistent, and their drunken minds saw the handsome nature of average men. She was interested in a night out with her friends, not in a one-night stand she'd regret in the morning. Unfortunately, she was the only one of her group who was not taken in by the group of blokes, and thus she was left to walk home alone. As if she was being punished for wishing to wake up without shame and disappointment.

She wraps her arms around her body, shivering from cold and fear.

Eddie speeds up.

Well, not Eddie.

Whatever it is that takes over.

It speeds up.

Until it's within a few steps of her.

And she glances over her shoulder and sees him.

She doesn't ask him who he is, what he's doing, or what he wants. She knows what he wants. And she runs. No hesitation, she runs, and the thing inside Eddie sprints, giving Eddie the pain of the surface against the soles of his feet whilst keeping the excitement of the chase for itself. He's far quicker than she is, and it doesn't take much effort to catch up with her.

Eddie's arms wrap around her waist. She screams as he throws her to the ground. She swings the keys she'd been clutching at his face. She misses.

He grabs her wrist and breaks it.

She screams again.

His fist meets her face. Hard. Again. And again.

And whilst her eyes are open and she is conscious, she is not aware enough to object or fight back.

Eddie's fist grabs a clump of her dress and he drags her across the road, into an adjacent field, and into the concealment of a bush.

It is here that his eager hands grab. They lift her dress and they grab. At no particular part, just everything, every part they can reach, every part that it knows will humiliate her.

It tucks Eddie's fingers beneath her laced panties and slides them down her curved, luscious thighs.

Eddie's face remains close to hers throughout. Heaving. The thing inside wants to see her face. Wants to see the pain. Wants to see how much it hurts to thrust that hard into something so dry and unwelcoming.

When it is done, it takes her over Eddie's shoulder and discards her in a stream that runs by the field.

When Eddie wakes up in the morning, he feels strange, but has no recollection of something sexual, no awareness of what he has done. He can feel the stickiness, but he puts it down to a wet dream, and thinks nothing of it.

He is blissfully unaware.

Completely unknowing.

No idea what he did.

The woman in question, however, wakes up as the sun rises. She isn't sure where she is, at first. She feels moisture, something wet, and realises that she is submerged in water from her waist downwards.

She vaguely remembers what happened. Images and feelings, a face covered in darkness over hers, the feeling of warm breath against her face, the pain of something inside of her. She knows what happened, but she doesn't remember enough to put it into words. No one looks at her as she walks home, wet and dismayed, and she does not tell her friends.

And she does not know she's pregnant.

Life is too busy to keep track of her menstrual cycles—she has a busy job and a busy social life, and she uses them to keep her distracted, anything so she doesn't have to think about what happened. It isn't until almost two months later that there is a moment at work where she pauses, a day where she isn't too busy, and she thinks—I've not had my period.

She books herself an appointment at the clinic, but never shows up. The abortionist is angry about the money he lost. She wants to rip the thing out from inside of her, but she doesn't have the guts to go through with something she has always disagreed with so vehemently.

She does it on her own.

Gives birth to it. Names it. Raises it.

Avoids questions about her father as much as she is able.

By the time the child becomes a woman, she has also become an orphan. Her mother's sickness turns out to be cancer. It ate at the inside of her for years, and by the time she goes to the doctors, it's too late. She hadn't noticed how much her body had deteriorated; she'd had something eating away at her insides ever since her daughter's conception, and her body didn't know any different.

Olivia was left alone.

After all, she did not know who her father was.

It wasn't Eddie.

Yes, it was Eddie's body. Eddie's penetration. Eddie's semen.

But it wasn't Eddie's essence.

Edward King was hiding away inside. He did not commit this atrocious act. He did not conceive this child.

The thing did.

And, as Mo takes his hand away from Olivia's arm, his jaw drops, recoiling at the sight of her, and he cannot hide his horror.

"My God," he says. "You *are* Edward King's child."

Nineteen

She drives like she's being chased. There is a fever to her body, full of sudden twitches, her glances erratic, at the mirror then ahead then her lap then the window then the mirror.

I can't watch her like this. I feel like it's my fault; my fault for telling her who she is; how she was conceived; why she never knew her father. But I shouldn't have been blamed for the burden of truth.

Either way, I can't let her keep driving like this, speeding across a dark, deserted country road, getting faster and faster; all it would take is for one of those sudden twitches to be a little too sudden, and we would turn into a tree or skid or flip, and she needs to stop driving, she needs to stop, and she needs to stop now.

"Pull over."

She ignores me.

Her breathing grows heavier.

She's panting.

Heaving.

She can barely breathe.

"Pull over!"

There are tears.

Her body is shaking.

Her arms, quivering.

Her belly, in and out, no sense to it, no rhythm to her breathing.

"*Pull over the fucking car!*"

She slams on the brakes. The car screeches to a halt, skidding a little, until it is stationary in the middle of the road.

I reach across her, turn the ignition off, and take the key. I put the hazard lights on—not that anyone is likely to pass us at this time of night—and I sit, for a moment, in silence.

She wheezes. Hands gripping the steering wheel. She rests her head on it, closes her eyes, but she doesn't calm down. Her entire body is trembling.

I go to put a reassuring hand on her back, but she flinches, and I quickly retract it.

"You need to be cool," I tell her. "You need to be calm."

"Oh, go to hell."

I know she is struggling. I would be too. I know this is a huge and bizarre piece of information for her to take. But, unfortunately for her, it's not the end of it.

There is more.

And she needs to know it.

"We need to talk," I tell her, trying to keep my voice low, calm, reassuring. "And I need you to calm down."

"When has telling someone to calm down ever meant that they've calmed down!"

"I know it's a lot to take."

"My father was conceived by Hell, you idiot—so what does that make me, huh?" She glares at me. "What exactly does that make me?"

I wish I could answer her, but I'm struggling to find the answer to that question myself.

How much of Hell is in her? Could she be the next heir to Hell? Or is the fact she was also conceived by a human going to stop it? Is she going to commit evil without even realising it? Is she possessed by this part of her? Or is it even there?

Most of all—what does this mean for the world? Are we going to have to fight the antichrist all over again?

I wipe my brow. Run my hands through my hair, leaving sticky perspiration between my fingers.

There is so much uncertainty—but there are also a few things I do know. That I can make an educated assumption about. That I need to tell her before we even think about trying to figure this out.

"I don't know," I tell her. "I don't know what it makes you. But there is more that you need to know."

"More?"

"I know." I watch her fingers stiffen, her lips purse, and I will myself to be patient. "It's okay, we can talk it through in your own time."

She leans her head back. Her breathing slowly calms. Her shaking becomes less aggressive. Her breath is still heavy, and her arms still quiver, but it is lessening.

A sense of lucidity rises in her—she is still anxious, I can tell, but she is at least trying to remain in control. I give her the time she needs, then eventually ask, "Are you ready?"

She snorts. "Am I ready..." she mumbles.

"You need to hear this, whether you like it or not."

"Fine. Go. What do I need to hear?"

I hesitate. Should I wait longer? Wait until she's more attentive?

Or is this the best I'm going to get?

"We need to keep Billy locked up," I tell her.

"No shit."

"Please, Olivia, just listen."

She huffs. Turns to me. Gives me an intentionally fake smile.

"Fine," she says.

"The thing inside Billy knows who you are now," I say. "It probably suspected who you were—but now it knows for sure. That means it will want to find you."

"Find me?"

"Yes."

"Why?"

"It will want to make the evil inside of you stronger."

"What evil inside of me?"

"That piece of evil that was planted inside of you when you were conceived."

"And how exactly will it do that?"

"By consuming your soul."

She closes her eyes and shakes her head.

"It will want to make that evil stronger, bring it out of you—and the only way to do that is to kill the human side of you. And a creature like the one in Billy—it will have ways of sucking out your soul."

"Sucking out my soul? Do you even hear what you're saying?"

"Yes. I know. It's..." I don't have a word to finish that sentence. Bizarre? Preposterous? Ridiculous? In the end I go with, "Surreal."

"So how do I get rid of what's inside of me? This evil, as you call it?"

"I'm not sure. We'll figure that out. But for now, you will not be safe so long as the thing inside of Billy is there. It will not stop trying to find you. At least he is locked up—at least we know that. It gives us a bit of time."

"So we need to exorcise it then."

"Yes, we need to exorcise it. But it wasn't responding

earlier, and it may not be so simple, and if we can't, well then... Then we must make a tough decision about Billy's life."

"Billy's life?"

"The last time that thing inside of Billy was here, it almost brought forth the end of the world. And with the thing inside of you, it has an extra advantage."

"This is so stupid."

"Edward King's bloodline needs to end with you, Olivia. With you, and you alone."

She looks out of the window. At the roof of the car. At me. At the wheel. Out the window again.

"Text me your address," I tell her. "Have some rest, then I'll meet you at your home around late morning, and we can figure out our next move."

"Fine," she says, so softly I can barely hear it.

"For now, why don't you let me drive?" I say.

She doesn't object. We switch seats and I take her back to the university so I can collect my motorbike; she insists she can drive herself the rest of the way home. I say goodbye to her and tell her to get some sleep. I'll see her in a few hours.

She doesn't say a word.

It Speaks

Billy is quiet now.

Shush now, little boy. Daddy's here.

The screaming is silent. The pain is unspoken. The misery is permanent.

He's still here, but he's taking a bit of time off.

For tonight, I have his body. I have his soul. I have his palace.

They lead us back to the cell. The screw ahead of us. The other behind us. Both acting like they are in charge, walking like big boys, swaggering, big bulky bodies, it's their prison, they are in charge, they have the power.

I can't help but laugh.

The one ahead glances over his shoulder. Scowls at us. His big, bald head; his fat neck; his thick torso he pretends is muscle, but we all know is fat.

I look at the one behind. Little. Scrawny. New. Thinks he has a promising career ahead of him. Thinks his life is worth something. Thinks what he does matters.

Big and Beefy opens the cell.

Turns.

Looks at me.

Expectant.

Waiting.

Impatient.

Hurry.

Not got all day.

I step inside. No intention of staying. Just teasing. Taunting. Enjoying myself.

May as well.

Why else would I be here?

He goes to shut the cell door. He can't. What's this in the way? Oh, it's Billy's foot!

He closes it harder. Trying to force it out of the way. I let Billy feel the pain. I hear him whining. Shush, Billy. It's my time now.

The screw's face curls into a snarl, lip curling, tells me to get in, slams against the foot again, superiority overcoming him, his fragile ego fully present. I'm going to enjoy butchering him.

Now, he says.

I take the foot away.

He pushes the door closed.

I barge it open.

It swings back, hits him in the side, and oh boy oh boy oh boy he is full of rage full of rage full of so much rage, and it is beautiful.

He charges at us.

I leap. Onto him. Legs around his waist. Hands on neck. Open mouth. Wide like when Billy went to the dentist. I throw our head forward, clamp our teeth on nose, and bite, hard, bite down hard.

Thick blood dribbles down our chin. It feels like warm soup.

He screams. Punches us. I'm impervious to it. I keep biting

and biting and biting and I eventually remove my head and, with it, his chunky, fat snozzle.

He screams and cries and shouts and breaks, feeling for the space where his nostrils once were, and I unmount him, allowing him to bash against the wall and clutch his face, desperate to feel a nose that isn't there.

I chew it a little. It tastes like rats. I notice Thin and Scrawny gawping at me, and I spit the nose at his innocent little face.

The deformed screw is torn. Does he retaliate? Does he grab the empty space in the middle of his face? Does he swear and grumble?

I take the handcuffs from his waist. Open them. Display the nice, sharp point. Thrust it forward. Land it in Big and Beefy's throat. Push it in Harder. Further. Until blood streams from the open hole. Then I take it back and survey the magnificence of the scene I've created.

He squirms at my feet. Writhes. Like a demented worm. Pressing on a wound. Struggling for breath.

Thin and Scrawny shits himself. Turns. Runs. I charge toward him on all fours. Leap onto his back. Take him down. He screams. I drag the sharp end of the handcuffs across his throat like a knife through butter. The wound spans the length of his neck. It gapes at me. Like the mouth of one of those muppets Billy's daughter used to watch. I leave him on the floor to die.

Prisoners look at me from the windows of their cells. Cheering. Whooping. Celebrating.

Begging me to release them.

I ignore the noise. Take the keys off this fucker's belt.

Run.

Along the landing. Down the steps. Open the door to the wing. Along the corridor. Along the yard. Back indoors. Almost at the exit.

A screw appears out of a door as I sprint along the corridor. I leap at him. I take this one's ear.

Another tries to stop me. It's half-hearted. He's scared. But his ego won't let him stand down. I shove the sharp end of the handcuffs into his naval and drag it upwards until his chest opens. His insides look like a butcher's bin.

I pause by the exit.

Glance back.

Enjoy the moment.

Open the door.

Walk into the night.

I am released.

And I know what I am after.

BEFORE

Twenty

It's 3:03 a.m. when he wakes.

He doesn't know why. It's debatable whether he's even aware that he's awake. But his eyes shoot open like he's been shot, and he sits upright.

Jennifer sleeps beside him. Breathing deeply in a gentle snore. Her lips part and an exhalation pushes a strand of hair away from her face. She wears a small nighty. The one she'd bought for their anniversary. The one she wore before they made love.

Billy turns and stands. He's topless, wearing only pyjamas trousers, and whilst his torso is sticky with perspiration, he feels icy cold.

Find the girl find the girl find the girl.

The words guide him.

He knows he must obey.

He knows he must follow.

So he does.

Like a soldier on sentry duty, he walks to the hallway and checks for movement. His daughter is still at her grandparents. Shame. He would have liked to play with her.

He marches across the hallway, down the steps, and to the front door. It's open. Ready for him. Waiting for his departure.

He steps into the night. A lamppost lights the street, but only faintly. It's a long street and there's only a single light, meaning there are many shadows where things could hide. Where things could jump out. Where things could do harm.

He runs.

His fingers stretched, his arms moving like a robot, his legs charging like an athlete.

Find the girl find the girl find the girl.

He runs.

...

Runs.

...

Runs.

...

He's in a church. He is no longer running.

He doesn't recall entering it. He doesn't know how he got in. It's the dead of night, and there is only a faint lamp in the distance.

He walks toward it.

Slow. Deliberate. His bare feet barely making a sound on the cold stone floor.

"Hello?" says a voice beside the lamp.

A vicar stands. Working late. Busy with thoughts. Aware that something is happening. Unaware of the despicable nature of what walks toward him.

"Can I help you?" the vicar asks.

Billy keeps stepping forward. He's thin and scrawny, but he feels big and bulky. Like he's a wrestler. A boxer. A fighter.

The vicar walks down the aisle and pauses a few steps away from Billy. He tilts his head and peers oddly at his guest.

Billy reflects the movement.

"My God," the vicar cries. "It's you."

Billy is aware of his thoughts, somewhere in the back of his mind—*What do you mean it's me? I don't know you*—but they don't reach his conscious mind.

In fact, he's not entirely sure where his consciousness is. Something else is in control.

The vicar turns. Strides. Then picks up the pace into a gentle run.

It runs too. After the priest.

Billy only has a vague awareness. He's drowsy, and he has no say on what happens next—even so, he is still aware of that same thought, repeating over and over again.

Find the girl find the girl find the girl.

He runs.

...

Runs.

...

Runs.

...

The vicar's house sits next to the church. It's small and quaint. A cottage. But there's room enough for the vicar and his family.

Billy does not know how he got in there.

He does not know why the vicar's eyes stare at him like that. Upwards, from his place on the floor. Blood dribbling down his face.

Blood.

From where?

And who are they?

The woman... The child...

Across the room...

Lying so still.

Billy looks up. Photos. On the shelf. Of the vicar and this woman and this child. Family photos. Together. On beaches. At theme parks. On benches.

Billy looks down.

So many still faces.

Why are they like that...

Silly boy, surely you know?

They are like that because the vicar wouldn't tell him where the girl is. Because he wouldn't give it away. Because he claimed he didn't know.

He probably didn't.

But that meant he had no purpose.

And the woman and the child...

The wife and daughter...

"Oh my God..."

Did Billy do that?

Of course not.

He couldn't.

He's not capable.

He would never.

But they are...

Dead...

They are dead...

How...

How are...

How are they...

Billy turns. Bursts through the house. Out of the door. Into the night. Past the graves.

Find the girl find the girl find the girl.

He runs.

...

Runs.

...

Runs.

...

"Time to get up."

He opens his eyes. The alarm clock is going off. Morning light forces its way through the window, uninvited.

Billy sits up.

Looks down.

At his hands.

Clean.

"You don't normally sleep through your alarm, are you okay?"

He looks up. Jennifer is already dressed. Smart suit. White blouse. Killer smile.

He's lucky to have her.

And that's why he lies to her.

"I'm fine," he says.

"Okay," she says, and kisses him. "Don't forget to pick up Tilly from school."

She walks to the door, pauses, and turns back to him. "Oh," she says, "and well done for last night—that was some good loving stud."

She winks and saunters out of the room, swaying her hips. Moments later, he hears the front door open and close. After that, a car coming to life on the drive, then growing fainter as it departs down the street.

Last night?

They made love.

Billy struggles to remember it. It feels like so long ago.

He closes his eyes and thinks hard, explores his memories, tries to recall the previous night's events...

Flowers. Meal. Tilly at grandparents.

That's what happened.

That's all that happened.

He rushes to the bathroom. Lifts the toilet seat. Throws up into the bowl. It's lumps and bile and blood. He goes to turn away, but another lurch pushes through his throat, and he projectile vomits again.

He slumps against the wall.

Closes his eyes.

Find the girl find the girl find the girl.

He opens his eyes, determined to see who's whispering that.

But there's no one there.

No one there at all.

NOW

Twenty-One

Olivia can't sleep.

How can she ever sleep again?

She's exhausted, but the tension seizes her body. She needs to rest, but the thoughts buzz around her mind like a swarm of locusts, and no matter how long she lays there, warm under the duvet in a cold, empty house, there is little she can do to force sleep to arrive.

She sits up. Rubs her eyes. They feel dry. She turns to the clock. It's just gone five in the morning. She's only been lying here for an hour.

She looks at the window. She sees the moon is sinking between the open curtains. The night is peaceful, but precariously so—there is a gust of wind, a few patters of raindrops, and it feels like the sky is threatening to launch a storm.

Her throat feels dry.

She turns. Places her feet on the carpet. The house is a new-build she bought a few months ago, and as new as the carpet feels, as fresh as the paint looks, as clean as the house smells, it feels unhomely. It's perfect but empty. New and unbroken.

She stands.

Walks across the room. Her legs are aching. She's not sure why. She walks into the hallway and doesn't turn on the light. Her eyes have grown used to the darkness, and the light would just strain them. She uses the banister to guide herself downstairs. Enters the kitchen.

She pauses by the fridge.

Looks out of the window.

A thin tree branch taps the glass like it's politely asking for entry. A few leaves dance in a circle in the middle of the road. The wind makes a gentle noise, reminding her it's there.

And she feels unsettled.

She steps toward the window. Searches the street for movement other than that of the elements. Half of the houses on the other side have only just been built and are unoccupied. Still, it feels like something is wrong. Out of place.

She shakes her head. She's just tired. It's been a long night.

Even so, there looks to be movement across the street. Yet, when she focuses her gaze in that direction, there isn't much to see. Only darkness.

Get a grip, she tells herself.

She's seeing things.

Whether it's from tiredness or a troubled mind, she's not sure. Maybe it's both. But she can't rely on her senses at the moment. There's too much confusion, too much terror whirling around inside of her.

She opens the fridge. Squints at the light. Takes out the milk. Finds a clean glass from the draining rack. Fills it. Puts it to her lips. Allows the liquid entry and relishes something cold against the inside of her throat.

Should she return to bed?

Try to sleep?

Give up?

Open the laptop and do some research?

Watch television?

For now, she finishes the glass of milk, swills the glass out with water, and places it in the sink. Turns to the window again.

There is a feeling in her gut, deep in her belly, a nausea, an instinct, an inkling—it tells her something is wrong.

She approaches the window. Rests her forehead against the glass, then rests her hands either side of her face so she can see outside without her vision being obstructed by her reflection.

There is movement.

Across the street.

Quick.

Her body tenses. Readies itself for battle. Shakes. Trembles. Gets ready to call Mo, and–

And it's a cat.

A small, black one, its eyes glowing in the dark, darting across the street.

She releases a breath.

Is that it? A cat?

She steps away from the window. Tells herself to stop being so tense. She's okay.

Well, she's not okay, but she's safe, at least.

She wanders into the living room. She doesn't make the conscious choice not to go back to bed—her legs simply decide to carry her into the living room. Despite the night, her curtains are still open; it's how she likes it. She turns on the television. Finds the news channel. Some bloke in a suit with greying hair speaks in perfect English about some debate in parliament.

Olivia laughs, then stops immediately.

It all seems so trivial now.

Leaders and politicians, arguing about this and that, debating the merits of one decision against another, ignoring their privilege whilst favouring the rich. It all seemed so important yesterday. Now, she thinks about how stupid and pointless it all is. They honestly do not know how precariously balanced our existence is.

She turns away.

And she sees it.

Something. Walking past her window. A figure, maybe?

She's not sure.

She didn't see it clearly.

Her body tenses. She trembles.

Should she run?

Confront it?

No. It's probably nothing.

A minute ago, she was scared by a cat. It's probably something else as equally non-threatening.

Still, she can't help the desire to check.

She takes a deep breath. Grants herself the confidence to face it. Steps to the window and looks out. Peers across the street. One way, then the next.

There is nothing there.

It's tricks of a tired mind. Anxiety creating things to make her scared. Terror confusing her.

Still, she stays by the window. Watching. Waiting for something to come back. For a face to appear, or the silhouette of a body, or the movement of another animal.

Nothing.

She walks to the front door. Ensures it's locked. Places the chain on for extra security. Returns to the living room.

The news has begun a different story.

One that makes little sense at first.

But she recognises the image on the screen. Even though she saw this man a few hours ago, it still takes a few seconds for it to register. But she realises it's Billy.

"Billy Tate, a man in prison for the murder of his wife and child, has escaped prison just less than an hour ago."

What?

"In doing so, he has left three prison officers dead, and a fourth in intensive care, fighting for his life. The police have released a brief statement, indicating that, should anyone see Billy Tate, they are not to approach him, but are to phone 999 immediately."

Three dead? Intensive care? How?

"Police have stated that he is highly dangerous and presents an immediate threat to members of the public."

Olivia turns back to the window.

Peers outside.

Every movement becomes terrifying. The wind becomes ominous. The flickers of shadow present an immediate threat.

Mo's words repeat themselves, like an echo from a deep pit.

The thing inside Billy knows who you are now.

That means it will want to find you.

It wants to consume your soul.

She wants to run, but isn't sure where to.

She wants to hide, but knows there is nowhere to hide.

And she wants to cry, but she knows it will be no use.

It's out.

It's free.

And it's after her.

Twenty-Two

Another vast array of stars; exploding planets lighting up the sky just for me. Just so I can lie here, beneath them, feeling calm, and thinking clearly.

Calmness, however, is much like the love of my father, or the affections of April, or any modicum of serenity in my life—it is something I cannot force, however much I might crave it.

I close my eyes. Allow my mind to rest. To wander on its own. To find solutions in its slumber.

What the hell am I going to do?

I should alert April. Tell her who Olivia is. With something this potentially catastrophic, she needs to know. The Church might wish to intervene. So why, when I'm usually so quick to provide them with such information, am I feeling so hesitant?

Because I don't trust them.

I don't trust what they will do.

Normally, an exorcism will end with success, and a victim's family will be delighted to have their loved one back—but not always. There have been times—only a few, but I know they happened—when the demon wouldn't leave; when it had amalgamated with the human soul for too long; when there was no way to remove it. Tough decisions were made. Decisions with the greater good in mind.

And those were just demons.

Whatever might be in Olivia was created at her conception. I can exorcise a demon as it's a separate entity as it doesn't belong in the body of its host—but whatever is inside of Olivia was born into her. It's part of who she is.

If they knew who Olivia was, where she had come from, what would the Church do then?

They'd witnessed the imminent end of the world during The Edward King War, when the antichrist almost brought civilisation to its knees.

They'd witnessed the imbalance of hell on earth that the Sensitives only just fought off; that the love of April's life sacrificed himself for.

Two close calls within a matter of decades after two millennia of peace... how easily will they risk a third?

Perhaps the situation isn't that bad. Perhaps this means nothing for the fate of the world, or for Hell's persistence in unleashing itself on earth, for its desperation to reign its dominance.

But would they take that risk?

No. They wouldn't.

The Church cannot know.

Not for now, anyway.

But April...

It saddens me to think that she cannot be trusted. That her loyalty to me will not come above her loyalty to the Church. Then again, she witnessed her soulmate's destruction—perhaps loyalty will mean nothing if it means risking such events occurring once more.

This leads to the only conclusion—that the burden of knowledge must remain solely mine, and I must be left to examine the grave dilemmas regarding Olivia.

How dangerous is she?

If the human in Eddie fought the Hell within him, then could she do it too?

Should we risk it?

I rub my eyes. My mind aches. I'm tired of these questions. I don't have solutions, and I don't expect any.

But I make one decision.

I will not let anything hurt her.

Not the Church. Not April. Not that thing within Billy Tate. None of it.

I will not see a person perish because of what may or may not reside within them. I've witnessed it too many times.

And, as I close my eyes and my mind wanders away, I remain resolute in that thought. It is the thought that guides me to sleep. The one that allows my thoughts to finally stop racing. The one piece of certainty I am happy to cling onto.

And just as I'm drifting off, I hear my phone vibrate. It's on its last dregs of battery, and I'm happy to let it die.

Then it vibrates again.

I try to ignore it, but the vibration is persistent.

I take my phone from my bag. Light up the screen. There are several messages from Olivia:

Mo?

You there?

Did you get my text?

Mo come on.

Her text?

I scroll to the beginning of her messages.

My arms tense. My heart punches my chest. Any sense of tiredness that was lulling me to sleep bursts out of me, and I read the message again to check—sure enough, it says the same thing.

Billy Tate has escaped.

Twenty-Three

She stops texting.
He's not answering.
And she needs to make sure she's safe.
Is she safe in her house?
Should she leave?
Is she safe anywhere?
Instinct tells her to stay. Where else would she go?

She runs from room to room, making sure the living room window is locked; the kitchen window; the back door to the gardens; the study window; and the front door, locked and bolted. She charges upstairs; her bedroom window locked; bathroom window locked; guest bedroom window locked; other guest bedroom window locked. Everything secure.

But the windows are still made of glass, which can shatter and break.

The front door is still made of wood that can be beaten down with a heavy shoulder.

And the locks are only made of metal, something that can be twisted and broken.

How powerful is this thing?

What can it do?

What is its strength?

She hovers on the upstairs landing. Considers her next move. The car's on the drive. But she's just locked herself in. She should hide.

But hide where?

She should stay downstairs. Listen for sounds. When there's a sound, she should get her keys and run for the car.

But what sound should she listen out for?

Every sound is deceptive. An owl outside. A stray cat crying. The patters of a late-night runner passing the house. These are all innocent noises capable of impersonating a savage assailant.

She drops to her knees. Makes herself smaller. That's what she'll do; she'll make herself as non-threatening as she can.

Non-threatening to what?

Jesus. Calm down. I'm sweating.

She's panting, too.

She closes her eyes. Covers her face. Then opens them. Wraps her arms around her legs. Stays still. Concentrates on breathing.

In, one, two, three, four.

Hold, one, two, three, four.

Release, one, two, three, four, five, six, seven.

This is what she does when she can't sleep. She's read about it. The four-four-seven technique. It's supposed to help you be calm.

In, one, two, three, four.

Hold, one, two, three, four.

Release, one, two, three, four, five, six, seven.

Right. There. That's it. Breathing is steady. Hands are relaxed. Arms are loose.

She's fine.

She'll be fine.

Just as the thought helps her fall into a state of relaxation, a clatter makes her body tense again.

It was over her shoulder. The guest bedroom.

Does she look?

Does she run?

Stop it, you're a grown up.

She looks.

Of course, she looks.

There's nothing in the house. She'd have seen it. Heard it. Any steps or smashes would have surely alerted her.

So she steps across the landing. Slowly. Edging forward. Staring at the door, cracked ajar, at the darkness inside of it.

And she reaches out a hand, stretching toward the door, as if her fingers are the brave part of her body checking it's safe for the rest of her to follow.

She places her palm on the door. Gives it a nudge. It creaks open. She turns on the light.

A book is on the floor. One about superstitious belief in Sumerian mythology. It must have been precariously balanced so fell off the bookshelf, that's all.

She lets her breath go.

Then holds it again as there is a bang on the front door. Three clear strikes. A stranger beckoning her to answer.

He's here.

She rushes to the hallway. Stops at the top of the steps. Stares at the door like it's going to explode.

Nothing happens.

Then the three bangs come again.

And there's shouting. A man's voice.

Could she leave through the window? Sneak out upstairs? She could run across the garden and get to the car before he catches her.

Yes, that's what she'll do.

The car. Through the living room window.

Only, she must pass the front door to get to it.

Deep breath. Let it out.

One step on the stairs.

Then another.

Slowly descending, not taking her stare away from the door. Should it burst open, and should Billy be standing there, she would be ready.

Ready for what, though?

To run?

Scream?

Focus.

Another step down.

And another.

She's halfway. The front door is coming closer. A slab of wood is the only thing keeping her safe.

BANG BANG BANG.

More shouting. Deep and gruff.

He's here.

Oh God, he's here.

She takes the last few steps quicker. She can't wait. He'll get in and she'll still be there. She must run.

Then the shouting comes again.

And she pauses.

That's Mo's voice.

It's Mo.

Not Billy, it's Mo.

BANG BANG BANG.

"Olivia, are you okay? For fuck's sake, let me in!"

Is it Mo?

Or is it Billy somehow pretending to be Mo?

Can it imitate people's voices?

She creeps toward the door and listens.

"Olivia!"

"Mo?" she says.

"Olivia, open the door, we need to go."

"How do I know it's you?"

"Because it's me, you bloody idiot—open the door!"

She weighs up the odds. Considers her chances. Evaluates the risk.

And she opens the door.

And Mo stands there.

"Are you okay?"

She gives him a vague nod.

"Get your car keys," he says, and she grabs them from the pot beside the door and hands them to him. "Come on!"

He grabs her arm and rushes her across the driveway.

She's almost at the car when she sees it.

And when she sees it, she can't move.

Not anymore.

She just can't move.

"What is it?"

Then he sees it too.

Across the street.

A silhouette below the lamplight.

Billy Tate.

It's here.

Twenty-Four

I have seen so many demons in so many people—yet it still shocks me how they can make a human look so inhuman.

The kind face, the wary eyes, and the downtrodden posture that makes up this tired man is no longer there—it's hunched, an arm dangling to the side, limbs askew, moving quickly with its joints shooting in wayward directions.

"Hurry!"

I get into the driver's seat. Turn the ignition. Olivia locks her door and pulls the seatbelt over her. She can't take her stare away from him.

I turn the car onto the road. Olivia lives in a cul-de-sac, and there is only one way out; the way that Billy blocks.

It remains in the middle of the road, stood stationary in the way of our escape route.

Do I drive into it? Do I risk Billy's life? Do I hurt him to hurt the demon?

I rev the engine. Consider going around it. Contemplate whether I'd be able to.

And I decide to go into it.

It's a risk, but it won't let me hurt Billy. If Billy dies, so does its costume, along with the entity's place in this world. It won't let me kill him.

At least, I hope not.

I put my seatbelt on.

"Hold on," I tell her.

She grips the sides of her seat.

I glance at the windows, scanning the windows on either side of the street. There are no twitching curtains, no lights coming on, no prying eyes. It is almost morning, but not quite—the time where everyone is still asleep.

I wonder how many people I'll wake if I make impact.

I rev the engine. Grip the steering wheel. Psych myself up. Will myself to do it.

It will be fine.

It will not let me hurt Billy.

"Fuck it."

I go for it.

Hit the gas, go up the gears quickly, speed up until I'm beyond the speed limit.

It doesn't flinch, or evade being hit, or attempt to dodge. In fact, it does quite the opposite.

It runs toward me.

Quickly—far too quickly, in fact, for a human—its arms bent and its legs gangly and its face a shadow of fury.

"Come on, come on..."

Move out of the way.

Please, just move out of the way.

We are going too fast to stop.

It's charging toward me.

Olivia is looking at me, then at it, then at me, then at it.

I brace for impact.

I scream as the collision is imminent.

And, at the last possible moment, when I think the plan is

going to backfire and I'm going to kill Billy—it leaps onto the bonnet and over the window.

There is a pounding on the roof.

I look in the rear-view mirror, expecting to see it fall onto the road behind me.

It doesn't.

I look up and find two sets of fingers at the top of the windscreen, clinging onto the car.

"It's on the roof."

I tell myself as much as I tell her.

I swing around the next corner quickly, fast enough that I might loosen its grip.

Billy's legs fall past my window, then climb back on top.

I approach another turning, speed up, and slam on the brakes as I spin the wheel and turn the corner at speed.

This time, Billy's legs fall past Olivia's window, then disappear back onto the roof.

"How is it doing that?" Olivia asks.

"I don't know."

I only have one more solution.

I turn onto a long stretch of road. There is nothing ahead and nothing behind—just parked cars on either side and buildings waiting to be opened for business. I have plenty of road to pick up speed.

I accelerate.

Harder and harder.

My foot all the way down on the pedal, going past sixty in a thirty limit, reaching seventy, then eighty.

"Get ready," I say.

Olivia's fingers grip harder onto the seat.

I pass ninety and approach hundred.

My face scrunches up. My hands grip the wheel until they hurt. My arms tense.

And I slam on the brakes, skidding across the road.

Billy's body flies off the roof, across the road, hitting the tarmac and bouncing further along.

I wait.

"Let's go," Olivia says.

"Not yet."

I must know if Billy is okay.

I want to hurt the demon, not Billy.

But the body doesn't move.

Should I get out?

"Come on!"

"Hang on."

I won't get out.

I put the car in first gear, anticipating our escape.

And I wait for movement.

"Come on, Billy, come on..."

And I have it.

Billy's head lifts. His arms push himself up. His body unravels.

What would kill an ordinary man simply wounds the entity.

And it's time for us to go.

I hit the gas and speed past it.

And it gives chase.

Faster than it should, Billy's legs moving too quickly for his body to handle—the demon will give Billy the pain, thus allowing it to sprint as hard as it is.

But it's still not enough to catch up with the car, and as I pick up speed, it grows smaller in the rear-view mirror, shrinking until I can no longer see it.

I keep going for another half hour without letting up on the speed.

I don't stop until I reach a hotel.

BEFORE

Twenty-Five

Huh?

What...

What is...

Billy's eyes open. His head is on the floor. In the living room. The ceiling is spinning.

He sits up.

He remembers Jennifer leaving for work. He remembers being sick. But he doesn't remember...

He stands. Checks the clock. It's half ten in the morning. He's late for work—they will be wondering where he is. Who will cover his lessons? Would they know by now to cover them? Should he phone?

He rubs his eyes. Sees his face in the mirror.

Shit. He looks like he's been dragged through Hell backwards. His hair sticks up in greasy clumps. His eyes look fully dilated. His skin sags, pale and grey, hanging off his bones. He looks like he's a lot thinner than he was yesterday. How is that possible?

He stumbles across the room, using the furniture to

balance, reliant on the sofa then a door handle then the doll's house. He reaches for the phone, then pauses.

A picture stares back at him.

Jennifer. Tilly. Him.

On a sunny day. On a picnic blanket. Cheese slices and ham and bread and crisps and mini sausages surrounding them. He is wearing a polo shirt and shorts. Jennifer is wearing a summer dress. Tilly is in her Elsa outfit. She refused to go out without it. He insisted she wore something normal, but she wanted to be Elsa.

It's a good memory, and he stares, mesmerised by it. By his wife's cheerful face. His child's playful demeanour. His eyes.

His eyes.

Whose eyes?

Find the girl find the girl find the girl.

The front door opens and closes.

"Billy, what the hell?"

Jennifer storms in, carrying Tilly in one arm and her schoolbag in the other. Tilly looks like she's been crying.

"What's going on?" he asks.

"What do you mean, what's going on? Your work phoned me to say you hadn't showed, Tilly's school rang to say you hadn't picked her up, and I've been trying to ring you all day to find out where you were, and you've just been at home in your pyjamas!"

"What? It's ten thirty."

"Shut up, Billy, you're not funny."

She walks past him, into the kitchen, places Tilly in her chair and starts searching the cupboards. She takes out Tilly's plastic plate and a tin of beans.

"I don't understand, I've–"

He notices the clock behind her. It's gone six.

How is it gone six?

He paused by the photo, and now it's gone six?

Tilly stares at him. Wet cheeks. He knows it will be difficult to fix that wounded look.

"Oh my God, I'm so sorry," he tells her, reaching for her cheeks.

Find the girl find the girl find the girl.

"What are you doing? Get the hell away from her!"

"What?"

He's not in the kitchen.

Where is he?

He's in the hallway. Upstairs.

What the fuck is going on?

"Do not touch us! I mean it!"

Jennifer backs up against the far wall. She grips onto their daughter with all she has, and places herself between Billy and Tilly.

"What do you mean?" He steps forward.

"Do not come any closer!" she screams, reaching a hand out.

"Jennifer, I don't–"

He reaches out a hand to calm her. There's a knife in it.

"Shit!"

He drops the knife. Backs away from it, and from his family.

There's blood on the knife.

He scans Jennifer. She's unmarked.

Has he hurt Tilly?

"Is she okay?"

"Get the fuck out of the house! Leave us alone!"

"Jennifer, I would never hurt you–"

"I said leave us alone!"

She grabs their child and drags her away, pulling her across the hallway.

He looks down.

His fingers flex around the handle of the knife.

He looks up. His family is gone. Darkness fills the window at the end of the hallway that was light only a moment ago. He's aware that time has passed again, but he's unsure how much or how little.

"Jennifer? Jennifer, where are you?"

He doesn't know what's going on. He's scared. He needs his family.

He walks across the hallway.

Tries the first door. Nothing.

Tries the second. Tilly's room. Nothing. Tilly's cot is in the centre of the room, her teddy sitting on the pillow. The one he built for her. The one she's long since grown out of, but doesn't have the heart to throw out.

He destroys it.

He smashes it to bits, furious that he can't find them, throwing it against the wall, breaking pieces of wood in half with his heel, striking it with his fist.

Once he has destroyed what he once lovingly built, he leaves the room.

Proceeds across the hallway until he reaches the last door.

He wants to leave them alone. Get out of the house. Make them feel safe. Stop whatever's happening.

But he can't.

Somehow, he can't.

Find the girl find the girl find the girl.

The cupboard door swings open.

He has the knife in his hand.

Except, now it's a new knife.

A larger one. A butcher's knife. Sharp. Lethal.

"Please…"

Find the girl find the girl find the girl.

WHAT GIRL?

WHAT DAMN GIRL IS IT?

STOP GOING ON ABOUT THIS GIRL!

He grabs the child.

"No! Please, no!"

He points his knife against the centre of her chest. She whimpers.

His wife cries. She begs. She pleads.

"Billy, please..."

He holds the knife beside his daughter's throat.

"Billy, no! Don't!"

The girl.

Finish it, so we can find the girl.

Hurry.

Lights flash.

His hands are bound.

He's in the back of a police car.

Neighbours stand behind police tape.

They all stare at him.

Why are they staring at him?

Where are they going to take him?

Quiet, Billy. It's okay.

Who are you?

A friend. I'm going to take care of you.

But where am I going?

To prison.

I can't... I can't go to... Why?

Don't worry. Their walls won't contain us. We'll get out.

And then we'll find her?

Yes, then we'll find her.

And what happens when we find her?

Oh, Billy, you are not going to believe it...

Why? What will happen?

Lights. Fire. Glory. The end. The beginning. Hell unleashed. It's going to be beautiful, Billy, I tell you.

Then we best find her.

It won't be long, Billy. Trust me.

You promise?

I promise.

Okay, then I'll wait.

We'll find her. We'll get her. We'll have our glory.

We will.

Once we have found her, there will be no stopping us.

That's right. Nothing will stop us.

Thank you.

Thank you for showing me.

Thank you for guiding me.

You are mine now, Billy.

That's right, I'm yours.

Good boy, Billy. Good boy.

NOW

Twenty-Six

The hotel room is as cheap as the price suggests. Bedsheets with out-of-date floral patterns, curtains with faint stains, and weak wooden walls. I switch on the bedside lamp, and a faint amber glow illuminates the faded material of the pillows.

Olivia is shivering.

She looks at me, wanting comfort. It's been so long that I'm not sure how to give it.

She steps toward me and puts her arms around me. She rests her head against my heart, and I place my arms around her.

We stand like this for a while.

My legs aching. Arms tired. Eyelids drooping. Remaining still, just standing here, content in silence, feeling the closeness of another person. I don't know if I'm lonely or if I like her. Sometimes it's hard not to confuse feelings with the repressed need for human touch.

"We should probably get some rest," I eventually say.

"Mm."

She doesn't move.

I realise we have nothing with us. No change of clothes, no food, no water.

It can wait. For now, we need to rest.

"We don't want to stay here too long; it's best if we get some sleep so we can keep moving."

I take her arms away from around me.

I look at the double bed. Wonder how we'll manage the sleeping arrangements. We need to stay in the same room for safety, but we also need boundaries.

I observe a chair in the corner. A sickly brown colour, with tufts sticking out of the seat. Still, it will do.

"You have the bed," I tell her. "I'll have the chair."

She scowls at me and shakes her head. "Don't be ridiculous, we can both fit in the bed."

"Trust me, I've had worse."

I turn away from her, leaving the closeness I didn't realise I was craving, and take off my jacket.

"Mo, you're an imbecile."

I turn around. Now she's smirking at me. Why is she smirking at me?

"Stop acting like the big macho man. I don't need saving from my own need for intimacy—I can handle sleeping in the same bed with you."

I sigh. "It's not you I'm worried about."

"I'm sure I can deal with it."

I hesitate. Go to object, but the look on her face is nothing short of defiant. There is no way I'm winning this argument.

"Fine," I say.

I take off my shirt. She looks at me for a second, then she turns to the bed, lifts the duvet, and climbs in. She looks away from me as I take off my trousers and climb into bed next to her, facing the opposite way.

And we lie like this.

Pretending the other person isn't there.

Putting a gap between us that feels unnatural. A space that feels like it needs to be filled.

I don't sleep. Neither does she.

And I feel a need; a desperate yearning; for her body. For her touch. For her closeness. She can give me the comfort I pretend I don't need.

I turn over.

"Olivia," I whisper.

"Yeah?" she says.

I say nothing else. She looks over her shoulder at me.

"What is it?" she asks.

"Could you..."

I can't say it. Can't ask it. Can't admit that I want to be held, that I am desperate to be pulled close to her but unable to conquer my pride.

She sighs—resolutely, rather than an irritatedly—and rotates until she is facing me.

She smiles. I hadn't realised how that smile makes me feel.

"Turn over," she says.

I almost object, but I don't. I turn over so that I'm facing away from her.

Then I feel her arm tuck around my waist and her body press against my back. It's so cathartic that I almost cry, and feel pathetic for feeling so weak.

But not so pathetic that I ask her to move away.

I relish every second. Every moment that passes by in the arms of another person; of a woman who knew without my asking what I needed; a woman who could have something evil inside of her, yet has the compassion to comfort a lonely bastard of a man.

My eyes close naturally.

My mind rests.

The warmth is more than just comfort. Warmth from a

human is different from the warmth from a radiator. It's beyond personal, beyond intimate—it's revolutionary.

When it occurs so infrequently, you realise how important it is.

And I fall asleep like this, resting in the curve of her body. Despite it being smaller than mine, I fit in it perfectly.

And she doesn't move away for the entire time we are sleeping.

Billy Speaks

I'm still here.

It doesn't listen to me, but I am still present.

Somewhere inside.

Tucked away behind the recesses of skin, slithering beneath vital organs, appearing when pain needs to be felt, vaguely aware and barely present, but make no mistake:

I am still here.

Only, I am no longer driving. I am no longer walking with these legs or waving with these arms. I'm screaming, but no sound comes out of my mouth. I'm begging for help, beseeching all who look at me, yearning for someone to look at these eyes and notice what squirms beneath the menacing veneer.

No one does. They'd rather think I am insane. Rather think I'm a murderer, than trapped inside my own body.

And I see everything.

It's a bizarre sensation, being so present yet being so far.

And I know everything it does.

I feel it.

All of it.

It's deliberate.

It knows I'm here, and it knows I have no control. It knows it can shrink me when it needs to, that it can give me the pain and keep all the joy; it delights in the torment of forcing me to experience its actions.

Like when it clings to the roof of a car.

When it swipes my rotten nails at someone's throat.

When it opens my mouth and lets my stale teeth devour whatever wretch has the misfortune to cross a creature they somehow believe is human.

I plead with it.

I'm hungry, so it is hungry.

And I plead with it—just feed on something else

And it does.

At first.

It hides in the gutter, placing my fingers around the hairy body of a rodent, digging my incisors into its greasy neck, ripping its head from its body, blood oozing down my chin as it grinds the chewy flesh with my teeth.

It doesn't spit out the bones. Or the eyes. Or the fur. It lets me feel every piece sink down my throat and into my belly. It settles uneasily, indigestible pieces of filth-ridden vermin swimming around the acid of my stomach.

It cackles as it lets me feel the discomfort.

And I beg it to stop.

And it says to me—*I was just trying to show you.*

Show me what?

What?

What were you trying to show me?

That there's a reason we dine exquisitely.

Dine exquisitely? What does that mean?

It carries me out of the gutter, away from the sewer, across the streets, through the darkness, and it lurks in an alleyway. They are looking for Billy Tate, so it uses the shadows to ensure our presence is unknown. When something has become so accustomed to the darkness, it seems like the safest place to go.

And it waits.

I don't know what for, at first, but it soon becomes clear.

It waits for a woman.

A straggler. Someone coming home at the late hour, staggering down the street, abandoned by her friends, left alone in the club, with makeup that made her look graceful in the early evening now making her look like a clown, limping as she struggles to remain upright in heels whilst so highly inebriated.

And she's on her own.

Please don't.

Fine, I'll take the rats.

If it means not hurting anyone, I'll take the rats.

It doesn't reply. Just laughs. Always laughs. I'm fed up with laughter.

I implore it to stop, but I can do nothing to prevent it leaping from the shadows on all fours and grabbing her by the ankles, discarding her heels and clutch bag. She's too intoxicated to struggle, and it drags her into the recesses of the alleyway; beside a cold, wet, brick wall; below the drips from the broken gutter beneath cheap flats; concealed by the anonymity of night time.

She tries to struggle. There's no point. She rolls over and a little vomit trickles out of her mouth. I wonder why she got so drunk, what is going so wrong in her life—but at no point do I blame her. She has a right to be as drunk as she wants and make it safely home.

Oh, Saint Billy, you are tiresome.

Please.

She's young.

Probably only just turned twenty.

Spare her.

I'll take the rats.

I promise, I'll take the rats.

It places my hand around her throat. My fingers look longer somehow, spindlier, like the fingers of a wicked, crooked witch. It presses down, squeezes. She chokes without struggling. The alcohol has already forced her body to give up, and her mind goes just as easily.

And I just watch.

Like a cinema screen I can't turn away from—except I don't just see it; I feel it. The flesh of her neck collapsing between my thumb and forefinger. The stickiness of piss and sick on her body. The putrid smell as her death forces her to shit herself.

And I thought this would be the worst part.

But then I am forced to eat her.

It moves my jaw, my hands, my arms, rips all her skin apart, tears it from her limbs, steals pieces like a ravenous thief.

It doesn't have to, but it makes me taste it.

It could enjoy the taste, the texture, the smell; it could enjoy it all for itself, but it doesn't—it gives me the terror of its flavour.

Because witnessing my revulsion gives it more pleasure.

Because my torment gives it tremendous satisfaction.

And I can't even use my eyes to weep.

I am in a vessel steered by something malicious. Something vile. It is the worst torment that could be inflicted.

Little do I know this is just the first.

No matter how much they stink, how full I get, and sick I feel—this is just the first.

In the morning, they'll find more than just her.

And we'll be long gone.

Hiding beneath the streets.

Lurking in the darkness.

Away from prying eyes.

Waiting to find the woman it's searched for since the beginning.

Waiting to claim the woman who will bring this world to flames, and to remove the man who stands in the way.

Waiting to open the woman that the Son of Iscariot thinks he can protect and unleash what's inside.

I finally understand now.

It told me to find the girl.

FIND THE GIRL
FIND THE GIRL
FIND THE GIRL

And now...

Now I think it's found her.

Twenty-Seven

Olivia tells me she wants to know more.
　　More about who she is. Where she came from. What happened.

She wants to visit somewhere that can give her a glimpse. Somewhere that will show her images. Feelings. Thoughts. Somewhere that will provide clarity.

I tell her I know just the place.

I step out of the room as she puts on clean clothes and wait against the bonnet of the car. I see another man doing the same further along the car park, engrossed in his phone. He lifts his gaze long enough to notice me, and gives me a roll of the eyes, as if to insinuate that we men must always wait for women. I give him a smile that I don't mean, and he returns to his phone. I intentionally keep my phone in my bag; I don't want to become a slave to technology like him.

Several groups of people leave the hotel as I wait. A couple with their hands together and their fingers interlocked, captured in a love-struck daze, giddy from a night of lovemaking, oblivious to those around them. Worn-down parents drag kids across the car park, telling them to put their games console away, telling them to pay attention, telling them to watch where they are going in the car park. I'm almost envious of the children, and a little angry at them—they have parents who care, who are trying their best despite being tired and fed up, and they show no appreciation. Ten minutes later, a man in a suit walks out, speaking on his phone, dragging a suitcase on wheels behind him. I wonder what important business meeting he is going to attend today.

Then Olivia emerges. Smiling at me. The epitome of sophisticated beauty. Dressed smartly, but without overindulgence—there is no need for her to compensate with her image for what she lacks in her intellect when her intellect is so strong. In fact, I can't help but admire her in a way I might have resented when I first met her; I am drawn to her resilience and intelligence. Yes, she was foolish to believe she was providing exorcisms to those who were probably in need of medical help, and she may have even caused harm doing it – but she is well-intentioned, keen, and unafraid. She knows what's chasing us, and she knows what's inside of her, and she is not running from it; quite the contrary, she is eager to gain knowledge and to add clarity to her understanding.

Plus, she's published a load of books. Anyone who has the discipline to persist with the written word already has an advantage over those who spend their lives wishing they could conquer the fear of mistakes that curse their creative potential.

"Everything all right?" she asks. I realise I'm staring.

"Yeah, fine."

"So where are we going?"

"To a playground."

"A playground? Why?"

"You'll see."

I take her keys and I drive.

She doesn't say much, and neither of us feels the need to fill the silence. It makes me think of our first car ride together, where the air between us was polluted by resentment; where she drove to the prison, seething with anger. Only a few days have passed, but the difference is drastic, and it astounds me that it's taken so quickly for the dynamic to change. I don't like people. I don't warm to them. Yet I find myself feeling more dedicated to this woman. She is more than a project—I am devoted to her safety, to ensuring she understands who she is.

I pull up beside a field.

I step out of the car, and she follows.

"So why are we here?" she asks.

I don't answer. I step across the field, a playground visible across the other side, and a flood of emotions takes me to my knees. I feel her fall beside me just the same, and I know she can feel it too.

She grabs my arm. I grab hers back.

"Oh, my God," she says. "What... what happened here?"

"This is where the final battle took place," I tell her. "This is where The Edward King War ended."

We help each other to our feet and continue across the field, the sun reflecting in the moisture on our shoes as we tread across wet grass. It feels like wading through water; the echoes of what occurred are difficult to move through. Everywhere I look, I see it. A death occurred here. A conquest occurred there. A demon rose from that spot. The events of a battle that took place decades ago, unnoticed by those who walk past with dogs on leads and children kicking footballs, lingers in a way that overcomes me.

For Olivia, the aftermath hits her twice as hard. I am a Sensitive, yes, but she has a connection to this. This is part of her history, part of her being—the same thing that made her caused the pain that occurred here.

When we reach the swing set, we stop. Watch it. I hadn't noticed, but at some point, her hand had found her way into mine. I don't let it go.

"This swing set..." she says. "Why... Why do I feel... I don't know what I feel..."

"I would guess, maybe, a sense of both overwhelming happiness and sadness."

"Yes. Yes, that's right. Why?"

"This is where Eddie and his best friend, Jenny, would come when they were growing up. When he had to escape his home. This was their special place."

"Where is Jenny now?"

"Gone. Eddie—or, at least, the thing inside of Eddie—killed her when she tried to save him. And this field is where it happened."

Her hand leaves mine to cover her mouth.

"And this was also where the final war took place, and where Eddie was saved from the evil that had taken over him. We can't know for sure, but Derek always believed that Jenny, wherever she was, played a part in that."

There are tears in her eyes. She fights them, but they are there. Because she sees it. Everything I'm saying plays before her like a bad piece of theatre.

She steps forward. Places her hand on the swing set.

And she falls to her knees.

I watch her eyes as they stare wide-eyed at the ground—but she does not see the grass before her—she sees death, blood, torment, mayhem.

But she must also see hope.

She must also see the moment he was saved.

She must see it, or there was no point in bringing her here.

I give her the time she needs. She stares, seeing it all, and I wait. Watching her, hoping this was the right thing to do.

Eventually, she releases the swing set and rises. She doesn't stop staring, not yet. That takes longer. But when she does, when she is finally ready, she turns to me, and she says, "Who is Lacy?"

I drop my head. "Lacy was Jenny's fiancé."

"Poor Lacy..."

Lacy was said to have shown up just as Jenny died. She must have seen it happen. She didn't want to be involved with the war after that, and I sometimes wonder what happened to her.

"I want to go," Olivia announces. "I want to go. I don't want to be here, I want to go. I can't..."

"That's okay, we can go."

We leave the park and walk across a nearby road as we return to the car, avoiding the return journey across the field. She remains silent, staring, her arms folded, huddled around her. She's shivering.

I go to put my arm around her, but she shakes it off.

After a moment, she says, "Sorry."

"It's okay," I tell her.

She drops her hand and reaches for mine. Our fingers interlock. Her grip is tight, like she's clinging on for fear she might fall away without something to anchor herself in this world.

We walk slowly past the field, and she doesn't turn her gaze toward it. She keeps her focus away, like it doesn't exist.

But I look.

And I see it.

Across the field.

The small figure of a man, hunched over, striding with a frenzy. I can't see the face, but I assume it's Billy.

It can smell her. It can feel her. It can follow the trace, and it will keep doing so, and we need to keep running.

"Come on," I say, and I speed up. We return to the car and

I get us back on the road as quick as I can without alarming her.

I glance across the field as we leave, but I can't see the figure in the distance anymore.

I drive away with speed, and don't slow down until we are far, far away.

Twenty-Eight

I pull up in the middle of blissful suburbia.

Children ride their bikes across the street. Mums stand at the window, watching their children frolicking. Dads fiddle with the open bonnet of a car, or assemble something with wood on their front lawns, exhibiting gender stereotypes in a way we like to pretend is dead.

"Why are we here?"

It's a fair question.

I point at the house I have parked outside of. It is the only house without a car on the drive, or flowers in the garden, or warmth in the windows, but even so, the grass has still been mowed, and the eggs that teenagers threw at the house on Halloween have been washed off. It has been minimally maintained to avoid sticking out on a street of families where an overgrown lawn or termites on the wooden porch might raise a few eyebrows, but is still clearly empty inside, like an urn waiting for ashes.

"Come on," I tell her, and I step out of the car.

A few twitching curtains show the indiscreet glances of neighbours in our direction. People on this street are not used to people entering this house. Their stares don't linger, however—these are middle-class suburbanites; the kind that will give a quick sneer then disguise it with a smile. They would never dare to ask what we are doing here, but they would certainly exchange whispers as we enter.

A small key safe is fastened to the wall outside the door. I punch in the numbers, release the key, and use it to open the entrance. We step inside.

It is immediately cold, and Olivia wraps her arms around her body. I consider putting the heating on, but worry about the noises a boiler would make after being unused for so long—I don't want this place to feel more ominous toward Olivia than it already does. A few days ago, she was an ordinary person, and whilst she appears to be coping well with the newfound knowledge of who she is, I imagine the balance between fake smiles and insanity is still precarious at best.

I lead her through the hallway to a study. I turn on the light and it flickers overhead. There is a bookcase full of ageing leather-bound books. I approach the shelves and scan the books, and it doesn't take long until the dust makes my throat dry.

"This was Derek Lansdale's house," I tell her. "Before he died."

She raises her eyebrows. Looks around with a newfound awe, her caution replaced by fascination at the potential of what she could learn.

"No one has lived here since," I tell her as she walks around the room, scrutinising every inch of the desk, every indent in the wood of the bookcase, and stops by the row of leather-bound books. "The Church feels it's a bad idea to sell the house. That too much supernatural warfare has occurred in Derek's name—that it would be dangerous to allow an ordinary occupant to live here."

"What are these?" She traces her finger across the top of the books.

"Those are what you've been searching for. What you wouldn't find in your university's library."

"What do you mean?"

"Your university wanted journals from Derek Lansdale—he worked there, so they believed they were owed it. The Church said fine and gave his journals to the university. Except, not all of them."

She grows increasingly curious. "You mean..."

"Yes. These are the journals the Church didn't want you to read. The ones the university doesn't know exist."

She looks across the shelf, pulling books partially out and looking at the dates on them.

"There is so much here I want to know," she says, reaching the books dated when The Edward King War ended.

"Take a few," I tell her. "Just not too many."

"Which ones should I choose?"

"Whichever ones you think will help."

"How would I know?"

"Listen to your instinct—your intuition will guide you. You're not just a regular person anymore, are you?"

She nods. Continues looking.

I walk to the window as she does. Look outside. Across the street. One way, and then the other.

Every face I can't see makes me alert. Every distant movement makes me concerned. I think I can see Billy for a moment, and I panic, about to tell Olivia we should go—then the person's face becomes clear, and it's just an old man hunched over his walking stick. It reminds me of the importance of vigilance, and I wonder whether we should be here.

This house helps Olivia. Helps our knowledge. Helps us to understand. But is it a sensible idea to go to a location where the supernatural is at its gravest?

Can the thing inside of Billy sense us here with an increased clarity?

And if it can feel us here, won't that propel it toward us with even more vigour?

"Pick whichever ones you need," I tell her. "We can't stay here."

She doesn't question it—for which I am grateful. Instead, she rests her hand on various journals. Closes her eyes. Listens to herself. I can't help but admire her willingness to accept what is happening. It's either brave or bizarre. I haven't quite decided.

She takes three journals and hands them to me, each dated shortly after the war.

"Can you put them in the car?" she asks. "I'm going to use his bathroom."

"Okay. Don't be long."

I take the books outside, looking around as I do. Glances from gossiping neighbours turn in my direction. It doesn't bother me. I block it out. It's Billy I'm searching for.

The entity can give Billy its pain. It could run here at speed by giving Billy the agony of fatigue, whilst feeling none of it itself. Which means it might not be far behind.

I open the boot. Put the books in. Close it. Lock it. These texts are important, and they need to be kept safe.

I return to the house.

Pause in the doorway.

Half in, half out.

Eager to go, and wishing she would hurry.

My hands find their way into my pockets. I look over my shoulder and make eye contact with a bloke watering his lawn. He quickly looks away. Oh, how I bet they've wondered about this house. How they've come up with stories, how they've debated, how they've disagreed: maybe it's deserted, maybe a recluse lives here, maybe it's even haunted, who knows?

Perhaps some of them have lived here long enough to have seen or known Derek all those years ago. They could remember his friendly demeanour. The last days when he was ill. The way he was a mentor to everyone he knew, whether or not he knew it.

Or so I've been told.

I hear a flush from upstairs. A tap running. The pipes make a groan as they are used for the first time in years.

And I see it.

The same silhouette I saw before.

The opposite end of the street.

Running toward us. Sprinting. Galloping. Hard. Harder than a human should.

Has he sprinted all this way?

"Hurry!"

I feel for the car keys in my pocket. I'm ready to race to the car as soon as she emerges.

What is she doing up there?

"Come on!"

A few faint steps down the stairs. "Sorry, I was looking at his pictures."

Billy approaches.

He's no longer a silhouette. He's a sweaty, bedraggled predator, smears of blood on his cheeks.

He's too close.

We won't make it to the car.

"Come on!"

She appears at the bottom of the stairs.

I get ready to run.

But it's too late.

He's approaching the car. He's blocking our escape.

I slam the door shut.

Lock it.

Bolt it.

Billy's body impacts with the wood, making it shake—and I know it won't be enough to hold it off.

Twenty-Nine

She looks at me.
 I look at her.
 Where do we go? What do we do? How do we get out of here?

I press my back up against the door. It shakes. Buckles. It is charging against the door, harder each time, making it tremble —the entity can pound the poor man's body against the wood as hard as it wishes; only Billy will feel the pain.

"We need to get to the car," I say.

I think I'm helping, but I'm not. I'm simply stating what we both know, but offering no solutions.

It pounds against the door so hard I'm thrown to the floor.

I rise from my knees, and it pounds again, and the edge of the door cracks, the wood splintering around the bolts that keep the hinges in place.

We consider upstairs. The other rooms. The garden.

It's no use.

It will find us.

Another pounding. The cracks spread further, and the top of the door leans toward us.

I grow conscious that there will be onlookers. Prying eyes from nosy neighbours. Twitchy fingers dialling 999. The last thing we need is police; we would need the Church's help to void any investigations, and I'm not sure I'm ready to tell them the truth yet.

Not when Olivia's life might be at risk.

I take the crucifix I wear around my neck, pull it over my head, and present it at the door.

"Fight it, Billy," I shout.

The door comes away from some of its hinges, and its face appears in the crack. It doesn't look like Billy. It looks like death. Pale face. Bags under eyes. Blood on its lips.

"Billy, you need to resist it."

Is Billy even still in there?

Has the *thing* eaten his soul yet?

Is he hiding behind the eyes, flinching from the pain, his moaning muted by the evil that dominates his body?

I don't know, but if he can fight, he might give us that few seconds we need.

"Billy, you need to fight it!"

It charges at the door. It forces the door break a little more, coming further off the hinges. I see neighbours through the gap, gathered at the end of the drive, phones to their ears. We can't hang round.

I turn to Olivia. Take her hand. I'm panting; I try to calm my breath.

"Soon as this door comes down, we make a run for it."

She nods.

It charges.

The door swings off. It runs at us. We duck, dodge past it, and sprint across the drive, ignore prying eyes, and get into the car.

I turn the ignition. Hit the accelerator. Ignore my seatbelt and drive.

He's in the rear-view mirror, sprinting past the onlookers, legs moving hard, inhumanly hard, painfully hard, and I feel for what Billy will be enduring.

But there is one thought that dawns on me—if it can give Billy the pain, that means Billy must still be in there.

I turn the corner.

A small car dawdles in front of me. An old man's grey hair sticks out from behind the car seat. Billy almost catches up.

"Bloody come on!"

The man is going nowhere.

I swing onto the other side of the road, fortunate that nothing is coming toward me, and speed up down the street.

I turn down another street, then another, and just as I think we've lost him, we turn down another, and are brought to a halt as the car meets a dead end.

I punch the steering wheel. "Fuck!"

No time to wait.

I reverse. Spin the car. A simple three-point turn. Move it forward. Turn it around.

And there he is.

Standing across the street.

Not moving.

Just hovering.

Hunched over. Panting. Dollops of saliva oozed from his lips, dripping on the tips of his worn-out shoes. The blood on his cheeks has crusted. He has already killed, and the longer we keep running from it, the more it will kill to survive.

Maybe we should just end his life.

But I can't.

It is not my decision to make.

I am not fate. I am not God. I have no right to intervene with divine decisions. I am a soldier, even though I don't obey commands.

And I must fight in His name.

I clutch the crucifix. Step out of the car. Ignore Olivia's protestations. Edge toward him, my arm outstretched, the cross between us.

"Let him find in you, Lord, a fortified tower."

It chuckles. Deep. Low-pitched. Croaky.

A sinister mocking of my words.

"Lord, send him aid from your holy place."

I step forward.

The space between us feels heavy.

Vast, yet small.

Dirty and clean.

Empty and full.

"Let the enemy have no power over him."

Each laugh is separate from the other. Pronounced. Definite. Drenched in spite.

"Billy, you need to fight this."

It looks over my shoulder. Leers at Olivia. It knows what it wants.

"Billy, please, if you are in there..."

It licks his lips. Flicks out his tongue. Stares past me.

"Billy, you need to–"

I hear the car door close and feel a presence behind me. Footsteps come closer.

Olivia walks past me, toward the thing.

"Olivia, what are you doing?"

She ignores me. Steps forward as if in a trance.

"Olivia, come back!"

She pauses. Steps toward it. Looks into its demented, desolate eyes. Twists her head to make her gaze more inquisitive.

"Olivia, this is what it wants!"

She doesn't respond to me. Her attention is focused on Billy.

"Who am I?" she asks.

Oh, Olivia, now is not the time.

She reaches out her hand. Rests it on the underside of Billy's chin. Lifts his head up. It grins.

"Tell me who I am."

It lets out a long, silent hiss.

"*You are the darkness before there was darkness... You are hate from before there was love... You are the evil from which evil was created...*"

My legs are heavy, binding me to the ground, the street magnetic to my feet. I want to help her, but I'm not sure she needs my help.

"*You are a part of me... You are owed to me... You belong to me...*"

Olivia twists her head to the side.

"*No matter how much you run, you are drawn to me... You are the true messiah... You are the one we are waiting for...*"

She shakes her head. Her posture is strong in defiance.

"And you are not real," she says.

It scowls.

"You are Billy Tate," she persists. "And I need Billy Tate to fight this. I need him to be strong. I need him to tell this thing that it's lost."

Its eyes grow wide with fury.

"*You dare—*"

It swipes its hand at her neck. She closes her eyes and prepares to be strangled, but the hand halts just before it reaches her.

The arm shakes. Trembles. Quakes.

Tears form in the corners of Billy's eyes.

His arm remains in front of him, hand reaching out, arms furiously shuddering, muscles quivering, reaching for her throat as something fights it from doing so.

"Go," says a human voice from Billy's inhuman face. "Now."

Olivia looks at me as she runs back to the car. I hear sirens. We need to hurry. I rush to the driver's seat.

We speed away, watching Billy as we pass him, held in that position, its arm out, its body shaking under the strain of battle.

We turn down the next street, keep going until we reach a dual carriageway, and speed away in the fast lane.

Billy Speaks

Please stop.

Just stop.

I hold its arm still.

The strain spreads pain throughout my body.

I've felt enough pain.

The agony. The anguish.

The constant running, the fatigue, the ache in my legs, how I can't run that quickly but it does it anyway, keeps going despite the torment, keeps carrying me forward, and I cry out and I beg it to stop and it laughs and I try not to beg, but if I don't beg, I weep, and I don't know which it finds more pathetic...

They drive away.

I hold my breath.

And I break under the strain.

Until they are gone and I can't hold it anymore and I let it go. Release the tension.

My arm drops.

Fuck you, you piece of shit.

Fuck you to Hell.

It laughs.

Stop laughing!

Always fucking laughing!

I drop to my knees. Cry, but it halts my tears. I want to go. I want to leave. I want it to stop, even if it means surrendering my body, even if it means giving up my soul.

But what then?

How many more people would it hurt without me to object?

How many more people would it kill?

I can't let it.

I can't.

It hurts, though.

I'm not strong enough to take it.

I'm not strong enough to endure this.

It's torture. Constant. No escape.

But I can't let it hurt more people, I can't.

"Hey, are you okay?"

Oh, no.

Please, no.

"Hey? Can you hear me?"

A stranger approaches. Kind face. Sympathetic smile. Older than me, but not old. Her hand on my back feels good. I only feel it for a moment, then it rips the sensation away from me.

It tells me I don't deserve it.

Please, leave me alone.

I try to say the words. I push them to my lips, force them out, but I don't hear my voice.

Please, don't.

Please, go.

It will hurt you, please, just go, just leave.

But still, she crouches over me.

Don't hurt her. I beg you, don't hurt her.

"Hey, how about we get you to the hospital?"

Why have you suddenly gone silent?

Your talking has been incessant. Your remarks, your insults, your degradation. Why are you quiet?

Oh, God. It's because of what you're about to do.

"Come on, we'll go in my car, I'll take you there."

It cackles.

"I'll help you up."

Her arms are around me. Close enough for my hands to grab her, for me to push her down, for my legs to mount her, for my thumbs to press into her throat.

Stop.

Please stop.

She's struggling, but it's too strong.

I push against it. Strain against it. Grind my teeth and fight it, fight it, fight it.

I throw my body to the side.

She stands. She runs. She flees.

And it's furious.

How dare you, you little troll.

Stop it.

You disgusting vermin.

I won't let you hurt anyone else.

It's time to sleep.

No, please no.

I let you see, now you can hush.

No, please no, I...

Silence.

I hate silence.

It's all dark. Blank. Empty. I don't know where I am, where we are, where it is.

Days go by.
No, it's just hours.
Or is it minutes?

It lets me open my eyes, eventually.
There's blood on my hands.

I'm in a house.
Her body is against the wall.
And it cackles again.

Get yourself out of this one.
Please, make this stop.
You can leave when you want.
I won't let you hurt anyone.
You did a hell of a job stopping me.
No—this is my body. My life. I won't let you.
Your notion of choice is an illusion.

You're doing this to force me out. To make me go. To make me give in. So I will give up and allow you to banish me from my body. But I won't.

I won't.
I will bear the pain if it means I can stop you.
I won't go.

I act defiant.

But I'm drowning.

It's suffocating.

Nobleness only gets you so far.

The pain makes you care little about others, and only for your own release.

And as much as I disobey, rebel, and endure, it's too much.

I'm fading.

I only come around now and then.

I can't stop it.

It will take her, and Hell will be here.

And I cannot stop it.

I know I will be gone soon.

And my body will be its vessel.

Please, help me.
I don't know if I can take anymore.

Thirty

Another hotel. Another room. Another bed.

It feels the same, but more tired. We walk in a similar door, but the legs that carry us in are more wearisome. We look at each other, not with looks of defiance, but with looks of hopelessness.

It will keep searching for us. And it will keep finding us.

And what then?

Truly, please, tell me, what then?

"Do you want to take the bed again?" I say, putting my jacket on the back of the chair. It's small, and there aren't any cushions. Still, I can deal with it.

"I don't want to take the bed," she says.

"Don't be ridiculous, you're not sleeping in this chair–"

"No, Mo, I don't want to take the bed because I don't want to go to sleep."

I look at her, unable to decipher her look. Is it exasperation? Irritation? Fatigue? Or is it a mixture of all three?

"We'll be fine," I tell her. "We're far enough away that it will take him a long time to get here, we're safe to sleep for now, but we'll have to keep moving in the morning–"

"No, Mo, that's just it—I'm tired of moving."

"I don't understand."

"I'm tired of running. I don't want to run from it anymore."

I huff. Not out of exasperation or annoyance, but for being out of answers. Honestly, I'm not even sure what the question is.

"Are you suggesting that we kill Billy?"

"No, not at all. I don't want to hurt him."

"Then what?"

"We can't keep running. I mean, is this what life is now? Hotel rooms and fast driving? That's not what I want."

"I'm not sure we have any choice."

"We do have choice. We have *a* choice."

"And what would you have us do?"

She steps toward me. Her fingers intertwine, fiddling. She realises she's fidgeting and drops her hands. She looks around the room. At the faded wallpaper, the sickly brown curtains, the disgusting floral bedsheets. Then she reaches her hands out to mine, takes them, and holds them between us. My heart beats a little quicker at her touch.

"I think we should fight it," she says, looking me deep in the eyes. Despite her sincerity, I can't help but feel she's being a little naïve.

"It's beaten me," I say. "More than once. I'm not sure I can defeat it."

"But it hasn't beaten me."

I feel a frown cross my face, and I fight it away. "Look, Olivia–"

"I don't need you to protect me. I'm not some weak little woman."

"I know you're not–"

"We've tried a sensitive against this thing, and it hasn't worked. But have we tried whatever it is I am?"

"You have the antichrist in you, it's not—it's dangerous to fight evil with evil."

"But I'm not evil."

"Of course you aren't–"

"And didn't it turn out Edward King wasn't evil?"

"Yes, but not until he'd murdered his friends."

"Then I'll have to do better."

"Look, Olivia–"

"I think I can do it."

"And what if you don't—what if it brings out the worst in you? What if confronting it just brings whatever's inside of you to the forefront?" She lets go of my hands and turns away. "I'm not running from it to protect you—I'm running away to prevent the worst evil meeting an even worse evil."

She sits on the edge of the bed. Hands on her knees. Staring at nothing. She stays still for a while, and I'm tempted to keep talking, to keep explaining, but I also know it's not the right thing to do. The right thing is to be patient.

But patience doesn't always work the way I hope it will.

"Then you kill me," she says, her voice small, and I'm not entirely sure I heard her.

"What?"

"If I fail, and he makes it worse, you kill me. You kill both of us."

"I'm not going to–"

"This is my decision, Mo. Not yours."

"With all due respect, this is far bigger than you."

"And with all due respect, this is far bigger than *you*."

I lean against the windowsill. Fold my arms.

I scald myself for even entertaining this ridiculous idea.

She is right. It is her life. Her body. Her soul. Her burden. Her choice.

Whatever is inside of her, we are yet to understand—if we

ever will—but it is inside of her, and this is her decision to make.

Then again, perhaps it's not.

When the ramifications don't just affect her, but affect the fate of an entire world, species, and way of life, then the issue is far greater. It is something that transcends human life or human values, something that is more important than either of us.

But what is the alternative? Keep running?

Tell the Church?

And what would the Church do?

Confine her to a padded cell? Demand her execution? Would they ever take the chance of her surviving after how close they came to losing last time?

It is a risk, but her breath is also a risk. Her heartbeat is a risk. The blood flowing through her veins is a risk. Every step she takes, every moment she lives, every waking or sleeping hour where she does not know what is building inside of her is a grave risk that the world cannot afford to take.

So no, I will not tell the Church.

And I will not force my solution upon her.

If this is what she wishes, it is what she wishes.

"Fine," I say.

She lifts her head. A look of surprise. She stands.

"But we can't do it here," I tell her. "We need to go somewhere secluded. Somewhere in a forest. maybe. Somewhere where we will not be disturbed."

I glance at the clock. It's almost midnight. I can't imagine many forests would be occupied right now.

"I used to go to the Forest of Dean as a child," Olivia says. "My mum would take me there on long walks. Sometimes with my grandparents. I'd run ahead and look at all the bugs on the trees."

She bows her head. It's strange how such happy memories can become sad ones.

"Then we'll go there."

She smiles. Moves into my arms. Holds me, and I hold her back.

And she kisses me.

Soft and brief. Passionate, but too short to put my heart and soul into it.

And we leave. Return the keys to reception. Then head for the car.

Thirty-One

We find the nearest forest and park in a small car park without defined spaces, the entry to which is barely noticeable along a country road lit only by moonlight. I don't bother paying for the privilege of parking here; I don't imagine a traffic warden will prowl here at this late hour.

We leave the car park, trek up the path toward the trees, and within minutes, we are submerged beneath them.

I let Olivia guide the way. We need to be where she feels most comfortable. Where she is content. Where she believes she can fight.

So I follow her. Her eyes remain straight ahead. Determined. She doesn't say a word. I watch her, walking a few steps behind, waiting for her decision of when to stop.

We have torches. A few lamps. The further we travel, the thicker the mist seems to become, until we can barely see ten yards in front of us.

Finally, she finds the place she feels most comfortable, and stops. She turns to me, nods, and we stand here, surrounded by mist and darkness.

We place a lamp on a log. One on a rock. Another on the ground. Another behind us, creating a square where we reside, illuminated by the faint grace of amber light. She takes a torch, as do I, and we flick them on, and we wait.

The cold feels colder tonight.

I've slept in fields and forests many times with only the warmth of a sleeping bag, but the cold has never bothered me before—but tonight, despite my jacket, despite my arms wrapped around myself, I am shivering.

She notices, and she wraps her arms around me. I feel guilty, like it should be me comforting her—it is she who plans to fight it, after all—but I say nothing. We sit on this log, her arms embracing my body, and say nothing.

She doesn't seem to mind.

Her arms are tight around me, and her head is resting against my shoulder. It doesn't just feel warm; it feels heavenly. I'm not sure if it's love or loneliness—it's so often impossible to discern between the two—but I don't care. I relish the touch of her skin, her forehead that brushes my cheek, her hands that rub against mine as she readjusts the position of her body.

I've paid women to give me less comfort than this.

We wait, huddled together, her arms fighting the shudders.

Animals make noises. Noises that, during the day, would signify the beauty of nature—but, at night, enhance our fear. Hoots from pigeons—or is it owls?—crickets hidden among the grass, cries of foxes calling for mates, the occasional steps across leaves.

We don't see a single creature, but we hear a symphony of predators.

The night grows older as we wait.

And we still say nothing, content in stillness.

There is nothing to be said, after all.

Sometimes, I think of conversations to start. Things I

could say. Encouragement or reassurance I could offer. Repetitions of the plan, as if we have one.

In my mind, I say it all.

I declare love and affection, wanting, and need.

I admit fear, worry, and depleting levels of hope.

I convey encouragement, faith, and belief.

But what do words do?

Words, even in their most amorous usage, rarely convey what silence offers.

So I let the night's hush talk for me.

I allow the lack of space between us to convey my affection.

I allow the noises of the night to convey my fear of what might go wrong.

And I allow our proximity, our closeness, my absence of words, to convey the possibility of success.

Do I think this will work?

Do I think she can do this?

God, I hope she can.

But I don't know.

I just hope she believes she can, and that her belief is not unfounded. Because I know, more than I've known anything, that if it comes to it, I cannot take her life.

I cannot go along with any wishes to cease her existence should the worst emerge from within her.

And as the thought arrives and leaves, we hear rustling.

A different kind of rustling to that of nearby animals.

Its stomps are heavier than an animal predator. More chaotic than a human. More ominous than a bird call.

She lets go of me.

Stands.

Straightens her back.

I do the same.

And we wait.

The stomps grow louder.

And I feel its presence.

It's the same evil I feel when faced with a demon, yet grander. More burdensome. More powerful.

She narrows her eyebrows. Puts on her war face. Prepares for battle.

Much as I have done many times.

There is movement in the mist, and the figure appears in the darkness.

It doesn't run. It walks. Slowly, toward us.

It knows we are not going anywhere.

It knows we are here to fight.

And it knows how foolish we are.

It reveals its face, demented and arrogant.

I glance at Olivia, then turn my attention toward it.

She takes a deep breath.

It is time.

Thirty-Two

Olivia steps forward.

I admire her bravery. Her gumption. Or is it stupidity? So often, the difference between the two is simply whether one achieves success or failure.

She has no crucifix. No weapon.

Should I have given her one?

No, she does not need one. She is the weapon.

She lifts her hand. Holds it out, palm toward Billy. Glares at him with an intensity one cannot muster without genuine hatred.

It concerns me.

It reeks of power, of authority, of domination, yes—but where does that hatred come from? Is it her courage presenting itself against the enemy—or is it something inside of her seeping through, manifesting, exposing itself?

Is it leaving her stronger, or more vulnerable?

Ready to fight, or more susceptible to being taken over?

I consider stopping the entire thing. Stepping forward, telling her this won't work, grabbing her hand, and running, far, far away, quickly, so that it can't catch us. I want to put an arm around her and protect her.

Whether that is from some need to keep us safe, to keep the world safe, or from an out-dated notion of chivalry, I don't know. Either way, I do not move. I remain behind her, watching intently, somewhere between morbid curiosity and deadly fear.

"Back off!" she bellows.

It steps forward. Toward her. Slowly, but not because she is successfully fending it off, but because it does not need to rush. It has time to taunt us. We aren't going anywhere, and its laughter mocks our plight.

"Leave Billy alone," she says.

Should I have given her the rites of exorcism? At least written down a few prayers? Is entering her into this fight without such knowledge like sending an untrained soldier into battle without a weapon?

It's too late now.

"I said leave him!"

It mocks her. Continually. It's laughter a constant noise.

She glances over her shoulder and shoots me a look. At first, I think she's worried—but it's not concern, it's an invitation. It's a prompt for me to join her, for me to help.

I retrieve the crucifix from my pocket and aim it in Billy's direction.

Billy steps into the light of our lamps—*it* steps into the light—and Billy's human features are all but gone. There is nothing redeeming about his face or his posture. It is entirely that of evil, that of something that belongs in fiery pits rather than pleasant woodland.

And I hope Olivia has what it takes to send it there.

"Leave this body!" she bellows.

"Do not keep in mind, oh Lord, our offences of those of our parents, nor take vengeance of our sins." I say the rites for what little it might help, my voice quiet beneath Olivia's powerful commands.

"Leave this vessel!"

"By Your name save me and by Your might defend our cause."

It continues forward, unaffected, cocky, like a stream of bullets have hit its body and simply bounced away.

"I said leave him!"

"Turn back evil upon my foes, in Your faithfulness destroy them."

It doesn't pay any attention to me. Its demented, fully dilated pupils are aimed at Olivia. Hands decorated red. Cheeks with crusted blood against dry skin. Pieces of flesh stuck within the fingernails.

"Leave this body!"

"For haughty men have risen up against me, and fierce men seek my life."

It continues, undeterred, and I try to quell my sense of panic.

The prayers don't work.

The crucifix doesn't work.

And Olivia, despite the strength and power and vehemence she displays, cannot get this thing to yield.

"Stand back! I said, stand back!"

"Because from all distress You have rescued me and my eyes look down upon my enemies."

It steps forward.

Passes the lamps.

Approaches us.

I remain behind Olivia, putting my trust in her, however misplaced it feels. Trying to keep calm. Trying to quell my breathing. Trying to tell myself to keep faith, no matter what, however hard—believing she can do this.

She can.

I really hope she can.

"Do not come any closer!"

"God whose nature is ever merciful and forgiving, accept our prayer for this servant of Yours."

God isn't listening.

Billy gains another few steps.

"I said do not come closer!"

"May the fetters of my sin be pardoned by Your loving kindness."

It stops in front of Olivia. Close to her. Too close. Passing her outstretched arm and pausing inches from her face. Its rancid breath makes her flinch—a reaction she quickly hides.

Still, she persists.

Still, she does not back down.

"Leave this man alone!"

"For He who consigned that fallen and apostate tyrant to the flames of Hell, hear our prayer."

Her voice is loud. She screams in its face. She commands it with all she has.

But she's too loud.

It reeks of lack of control. It does not display the might she wishes it to, but shows how untrained and out of her depth she is.

And I fear for the worst.

"Leave Billy's body!"

"Hasten to our call for help and snatch from ruination this noonday devil."

Her voice breaks under the strain, its defiant face an inch away from hers.

It basks in it.

It lifts its head and grins.

It rejoices in her trivial efforts.

"Leave!"

"Strike terror, Lord, into the beast now laying waste in Your creation."

It ignores us and, instead of backing down, it reaches its cold hands out and clamps them around Olivia's arms.

It makes contact with her skin and, in doing so, ensures that she sees exactly what it wishes her to see.

Thirty-Three

A red eye casts itself over the land.

Forests, fields, roads, paths, houses, homes, buildings, schools, towers, cities, countryside—every single thing we know to be part of our human world is gone and cast to unending fire.

Nothing survives.

No memories. No objects. No hope.

They cast you out of your home as it burns to the ground, only to find more fire destroying the street your children used to ride their bikes down.

But the fire does not kill you.

It's not a fire that comes from this world.

It's a fire that catches you, grips you, licks you, holds you—but never lets you die. You remain in permanent torment, forever burning to death, but never having the sweet release of your life's end.

Those that aren't swallowed by the fire are captured by beasts with multiple heads, parts of animals melded together in unthinkable ways, every biblical fear come true, every image of Hell nowhere near bad enough for what is unleashed.

Those who are caught first are hung from the cliffs, left dangling from a mountain by rope. Their suffocation lasts thrice as long, and their presence is a permanent reminder to any surviving humans that death only awaits the fortunate.

Rain is fire.

Sleet is fire.

Snow is fire.

It hits us like a barricade, a storm with tsunamis of flames, battering through this world, destroying five thousand years of civilisation in the time it takes The Devil to grin.

Volcanos rise through the ground, every dormant pit of lava spewing its wrath down the cliffs and through the towns.

For demons, our Hell is their Heaven.

They are no longer trapped below, only able to torture the sinful, constantly needing to battle to earth through the prison of susceptible human vessels. Weak flesh no longer constrains their attempts to enter this world, they can emerge as they wish, and they can dance on the flames, kicking them like a child in the sea.

You watch your loved ones suffer while you suffer.

You watch your children fucked by claws and your wives stripped by fangs and your husbands sodomised by horns.

You watch the world burn and know that the excruciating agony you can barely endure for the forthcoming seconds will last all eternity.

Your pain is their pleasure.

The world you were so arrogant to claim as your own is no longer yours. You must give it up to the creatures you were never sure existed.

Hell has opened, and the world has faced the consequences.

And where is Heaven in all this, you ask?

The Heaven that refused to meddle with human life,

whilst Hell, without the moral restrictions of the divine, tampered with it for pleasure?

The Heaven that did not answer your prayers when you battled this evil?

They are away. Scared. Helpless.

It's too late for their intervention. By definition, they are moral and cannot intervene; they granted the human race free will, and this is where our free will has led us.

The world has ended, a new one has begun.

And it is a beautiful disaster for every demon to enjoy.

And, as Billy's cold hands leave Olivia's arms, she understands. It has shown her what the world might be if what is inside her wins.

She understands the risk.

She knows what it is after.

Thirty-Four

She's on her knees, so still it feels like she's not real.

"Olivia?"

Her head flinches, but it's all the reaction I get.

She stares at the ground, caught between shock and dismay. She looks fragile. Like a dormant bomb. Empty, not because she cannot feel, but because all feelings have drained from her.

It showed her something.

Something bad.

Something horrific.

And, as it approaches her, it has her right where it wants her. It doesn't hurry—it doesn't need to—it simply saunters toward her with a slow, cocky stride, licking its lips, stretching its fingers.

I step forward. Thrust my crucifix toward it.

It's just the eye of her storm. She'll get up in a moment, and she'll be ready, full of vigour, ready to fight—I know she will. I must count on her; I must have faith in her. I just need to bide time; she will get up; she will continue fighting.

Won't she?

"Almighty God who gave to Your holy apostles the power to tramp underfoot serpents and scorpions."

Words that would give me the strength to command a demon only give me a vulnerability that appears pathetic to an entity of pure evil. It does not stop walking forward. In fact, if anything, my words seem to spur it on.

"I humbly call on Your holy name and pardon my sins."

It stops in front of my crucifix.

Looks at it like I'm offering a lollipop.

Tilts its head, inquisitive, curious as to what I think it can do.

Come on Olivia.

"I ask that You grant me, Your unworthy servant, the power to confront and compel this beast."

It grabs my wrist and pulls the crucifix toward it, presses it against Billy's chest, and smoke rises from his skin, the smell of fumes, the hissing of burning.

I am unsure what to do—do I keep the crucifix here as my only armour, or do I pull it away to save Billy the pain?

I glance over my shoulder. Olivia hasn't moved. I need her to move.

"Come on, Olivia, I need you!"

She decided to do this. She thought she had the power to fight it. She was convinced this was the best option.

And now she's left me to do battle with something I cannot control, and I am struggling – truly struggling – to get any kind of hold on this creature.

"I ask through You to make judgement on both the living and the dead and the world through fire."

My voice is soft, and my words are unconvincing.

It pulls the crucifix harder against Billy's chest, leaving an imprint on Billy's skin, and it reaches out a hand, places it on the underside of my chin, and drags its fingers down my neck.

"Olivia!"

Its thumbs squeeze my throat.

I struggle to breathe.

But I persist with the rites of exorcism, despite them being useless, despite my words barely passing my lips under the pressure of its grip.

"I appeal to Your holy name, humbly begging your kindness, that You graciously grant me help against this unclean spirit."

It squeezes harder, and I can't speak, can't breathe.

I try stepping backwards, moving out of its reach, but it walks with me.

I remove the crucifix and try punching its arm away, but it's firm, strangling me, humiliating me.

I keep stepping backwards.

It keeps moving with me.

Then my legs collide with Olivia's crouched body, and I fall over her, and it is forced to release me.

I choke. Grab my neck. Wheeze. Breathe in as much air as I can.

Olivia's head rises, slightly, hair over her eyes, concealing her torment. I cannot see whether there is fear or resolve.

"Olivia, I need your help, please."

Her head turns to me.

It stands over her. Flexing its fingers.

Ready.

For what, I don't know.

But it will be both devastating to her life, and to this world.

"Olivia—it showed you a glimpse, that is all."

Her eyes lock on mine.

It showed her something awful.

And she cannot come to terms with it.

"It only showed you its fantasy," I persist. "Just an image of what could be, that is all. You can change it."

It reaches its hands toward her.

I grab her face. Turn it toward mine. Lock onto her eyes and hope to God that she listens to me.

"If it can show you something, you must also have the power to show *it* something."

Her eyebrows narrow. She looks curious. Like my words have resonated with her. Like they mean something.

Like she has an idea.

Its hands land on her head.

She grabs its wrists.

Clamps down with both fists.

And she stands.

It struggles, trying to release itself from her grip.

It can't.

She strides, forcing it to walk backwards. Glaring at its destroyed visage.

She takes it to the ground.

And this time, she shows it what she wants it to see.

Billy Speaks

My chest still burns.

I can still feel the outline of the crucifix embedded into my skin.

Once, I took a tray of cookies out of the oven without oven gloves—the two seconds my fingers held that oven tray stung like hell—the crucifix on my chest felt like that, but longer. And, even though the crucifix is now gone, the burning still swells and intensifies.

But I can't allow it to lessen my resolve.

I can see them, trying to help me.

And I can see her standing over me.

She grips my wrists, looks into my eyes, and takes me to the ground, falling, and I expect my head to make an impact and to feel the most intense pain—but I don't.

In fact, I feel nothing.

I'm suddenly somewhere else.

Like a blank room, but not. To say it's a room would be to impose human rules on it, and it's not a human situation—similarly, to say it's blank would be to suggest something once existed to fill it, and it feels too light to be ever have been full.

It is nowhere and everywhere. Just a place; somewhere else; somewhere a human is not usually permitted.

Is this death?

Has the thing finally banished me from my body?

Am I now in Purgatory?

"You're not dead."

I turn around.

She stands there.

Still, and full of grace. There is no sweat on her skin, no hair over her face, no terror in her eyes. The woman who's been battling to save me is here, but she doesn't look like she's been in battle.

"What's going on?" I ask.

"I need you to fight it."

I bow my head.

Oh, if only she knew how I'd tried.

Over and over, I've begged it, pleaded with it, compelled it, and it's never listened.

"Begging won't do anything."

I look at her curiously. Can she read my mind?

"You've been asking it. Stop asking it. Start telling it."

"It's too strong. I can't make it do anything."

She steps toward me.

"You owe it to *them* to fight."

"Huh?"

"This thing killed *them*."

"I don't–"

She puts her hand on my chest, and the second her palm makes impact, I am transported, far away, to a place more familiar.

It is a kitchen.

My kitchen.

I'm cooking.

I have an apron on.

A pan on the stove.

And I am graced with the sound of small bare feet patting along the kitchen floor.

It can't be.

I turn. It's my daughter.

I go to my knees and wrap my arms around her, hold her tight, unable to help the tears, unable to find the words.

I thought I'd never see her again.

I thought it would never happen.

I thought it had killed her—I thought *I* had killed her.

"Daddy, you're squeezing me too tight!"

Her voice is playful and happy. I stop hugging and hold her in front of me so I can have a good look at her.

She's wearing the t-shirt I bought her. It's purple, with a picture of a unicorn on, a big smile on its face.

This is familiar.

This isn't real.

It's a memory.

I remember…

I was cooking tea because my wife was stuck at work. I was making sure she had something waiting for her when she came home. My daughter was doing art in the living room and had come in to tell me something…

I can't remember what she came to tell me…

I struggle to clutch the memory, it falls between my fingers like water, I try to hold onto it, I can't, and my daughter is gone—gone again—and now I am in our bedroom.

I'm looking down at my bloody hands.

My daughter and wife are below me.

Their bodies are below me.

And I don't understand.

Who did this?

Did I do this?

How did I do this?

I would never do this.

Ever.

"The thing inside of you did it."

Her voice.

I turn around and she's there.

Standing by the bedside lamp we bought from an antiques shop. And the bed where we conceived our daughter. And in the room where my family was murdered.

"But I..." I look down at my hands; if I didn't do this, how are my hands covered in so much blood?

"Because it wants to torment you," she tells me. "And now it wants you to take more lives."

"I—I can't stop it."

She steps toward me. "Who else can?"

"I... Not me... I can't..."

"Stop asking it. Start telling it."

"But I–"

"Look at what it's done!" She's shouting now. "Look at what it made you do!"

I look down at my family.

My child's face.

So still.

Staring ahead like she's shocked.

My wife beside her, unable to protect her, unable to keep her safe from my hands.

My hands...

Those hands that once held my daughter's; made objects out of clay with her; coloured in with her; fed her when she was a baby; stroked her hair when she cried; lifted her onto my shoulders when her legs were tired.

And now... The things it's made me do with these hands...

I feel a sickness in my stomach.

I haven't felt anything in my stomach for so long, but now I do. It's a queasiness—a mixture of nerves and fury—and it rises through me, lurching up my throat, poisoning my mind with strength.

I'm back in the forest.

She releases my hands and stands up. Looking down at me. At us.

And I am here.

Not just in the backseat—I am here, fighting for control.

It defies me.

It refuses me.

It commands me to return to my subservience.

But I don't. I will not.

This is my body. My life. My hands.

And you will not take it.

Thirty-Five

She lets go of his arms.
Something changes.
She stands back. I stop the rites. And we wait.

It—or Billy, I can't tell—is still. Motionless for a moment. Its eyes torn somewhere between wrath and vulnerability. Billy's eyes become his own, but only fleetingly, brief glimpses of the man that remains somewhere inside.

He shakes.

And he collapses.

He writhes on the floor, squirming and grabbing, wriggling and clutching. His limbs stiffen in one direction, then the other. His arms point in obscure directions, waving back and forth, fingers pointing then bending.

Foam comes out of his mouth.

To most, this would look like a seizure. To the trained observer, it looks like an internal war.

We kneel beside him. I place my hand on the back of his head and keep it there, ensuring he doesn't strike it against the ground, making sure he doesn't get an injury he can't recover from.

Olivia, meanwhile, tries to take his hand—but the hand won't stay still—so she places her hand on his heart instead.

"It's okay, Billy," she says, her voice soft and soothing. "It's okay, we're here."

It screams. Half a screech, half a cry. The demon squeals, then the moan is prolonged into a man's roar.

"You can do this," Olivia tells him. "Keep fighting, you're getting there."

But it doesn't look like he's getting there.

It looks like Billy is emerging—even occasionally surfacing—but the demon is fighting just as much as Billy is—both of them battling for his body—for his soul.

"You're doing great, Billy—I know it hurts, just keep going, and it will all be over soon."

I glance at her. Wondering how she knows this.

"You're doing well, keep fighting."

It shouts, a cry of pain entwined with words, *You fucking bitch* melded with a man's groan, growing louder into *Get out of me get out of me!*

The writhing becomes more furious, the seizure makes his body bolt, his arms and legs shooting in wayward directions, his neck turning his head unnaturally to the side. I struggle to keep his head safe, to keep him from hitting his cranium against the ground; the demon even lifts its head and tries to strike backwards against the ground, but I keep my hands there, struggle as I might, I keep them there, keeping his head safe, keeping him going.

There is warfare going on inside this body, and it is unclear which side will win—but it is something we have little control over.

So we do what we can.

I protect his head, and Olivia keeps talking.

"I know you can do this, I know you're strong enough."

Nnnnnnnnyyyyyeeeeeeeenooooimnoooooot...

"Yes you are! You've endured so much already, and this is it, the last bit, you can do this, Billy, you can do this."

An even louder scream echoes around the woodland and dozens of birds bat their wings in response, a flock fleeing for a safer tree.

She takes her hand from his heart and places it on his cheek. Looks deep into his eyes, seeing both the man and the monster, and wills him to keep going.

"Come on, Billy, come on..."

NnnnnnyyyoooooIcanttakeanymooooooore...

"Yes you can, Billy, yes you can."

He shakes his head furiously.

It grins.

Unwilling to relent, to let this man go, to let this thing win, Olivia mounts Billy's body, her legs either side of his belly, and pins his arms down.

They fight against her, but she matches its strength.

Whatever is inside of her matches its strength.

"Come on!"

It twists and turns and fidgets and fights, but she persists, holding it still, peering into Billy's eyes with calm sincerity.

"Think of your family, Billy."

He is still for a moment.

He looks up at her.

His lip curls. His defiance shows. He screams harder.

And harder.

And harder.

And the thing screams with him, human and inhuman voices combined, the noise unbearable.

"Come on, Billy!" she shouts, though the words are lost.

His screams cease.

His body grows still.

He is frozen in one position, eyes wide, staring upwards, body unmoving.

Is he breathing?

I can't tell if he's breathing.

Olivia places her fingers on the side of his neck.

He definitely isn't breathing.

"Come on, Billy, don't die."

But he doesn't move.

His chest doesn't rise.

His eyes don't flicker.

"Come on, Billy!"

Still nothing.

Not a flinch.

She opens his mouth, pinches his nose, and moves her head over his, aligning their mouths for CPR.

But something happens just before her mouth reaches his.

Billy's body trembles, ever so slightly, and something rises from between his lips.

Something dark, made of smoke and fire and wind and blackness.

And it travels toward Olivia's open mouth, where it seems to hover around her lips, poised and waiting, then circles the inside of her mouth.

Whatever it is, it hits her hard, and she falls to her back.

Billy sucks in a series of sharp gasps of air.

I rush to Olivia's side.

For a moment, I think she's dead.

Then she turns her head to me and says, in a quiet voice, "Did I do it?"

Billy sits up. His face is wounded and scarred, but with human features. He looks around, confused, then sees Olivia, and seems to recognise her.

Olivia takes my hand in hers and clutches it.

"You did," I tell her. "You did."

Statement from UK Prison Service

The search for escaped convict Billy Tate, currently serving two life sentences for the killing of his wife and child, ended today.

Tate, who murdered three prison officers in his escape, gave himself up in the early hours of the morning, and is now being detained in an undisclosed prison. Following an appeal from his lawyers, a judge agreed that Tate is mentally unfit to continue his sentence in prison, and he will shortly be moved to a highly secure mental health facility pending further examination.

Henry Myers, the prison warden of the facility Tate escaped from, said today that he is keen for there to be a thorough investigation into how Tate was able to escape. "We have lost three good men—three members of our prison officer family—and I will welcome the verdict for whatever scrutiny the prison is put under."

Myers went on to pay tribute to "three of the best, most dedicated men I knew." The police have not yet confirmed whether any members of the public were harmed in the few days when Tate had escaped from incarceration.

Following the suggestion that Tate claimed to be 'demonically possessed,' and rumours that the prison had allowed exorcists in to treat him, a spokesperson for the Church of England labelled such accusations as "ludicrous" and "rubbish", stating that exorcisms were rarely carried out in modern times.

More updates to follow.

Thirty-Six

This morning, I feel lighter.

It could be a relief that it's over.

It could be the sun shining through the windows.

Or it could be the naked woman beside me. Who am I to know?

I rub my eyes. Look at her alarm clock. It's just gone seven. I seem incapable of sleeping beyond this point—I've spent too many nights slumbering beneath the stars only to be woken by the sunrise, and now I struggle to sleep beyond it.

She turns over and looks at me. Her eyes have barely opened, and she still looks tired. She snuggles her body closer to mine, and she feels warm.

"Hey," she says.

"Hey."

"Would you like a coffee?"

"I'll go make them."

"No, it's my house, I'll–"

"Please, I'll go make it."

She's still weary. Tired from what happened a week ago.

Every now and then, she'll move and groan, or she'll rub her sinuses to quell a headache. She doesn't say it much, but whatever happened between her and Billy in those final moments—where she seemed to suck the thing out of him to get rid of it—it has taken a lot out of her.

I kiss her forehead, sit up, and turn until my feet touch the carpet. I put on some underwear, stand, and stretch.

She's watching me.

So I give her a smile.

"Hurry back," she says, and it feels strange to be wanted.

Dad didn't want me.

April didn't want me.

Hookers only pretended to want me.

And to have this woman, intelligent and remarkable, laying in a bed she's welcomed me to, asking me to return to bed quickly, seems quite surreal.

Despite all the demons I've battled, this is the most unearthly sensation I know.

I go downstairs and into the kitchen. I lift the blind and let the morning sun grace the room. Every surface is clean, every tile is spotless. It's not what I'm used to.

She has a coffee machine. I pour some coffee beans into it, press a few buttons, and it makes a grinding noise. I assume it's working. I pour some milk into two mugs and I lean against the side, looking out of her garden doors at a patch of grass surrounded by trees and bushes. There is a bird feeder in the centre of the garden, and a flower bed to the left. It feels like a garden that belongs to a family, not to a woman who lives here on her own.

The grinding on the machine stops, and the sound of trickling starts. I assume it still hasn't finished.

I feel a prick of coldness, but it leaves quickly. The sun casts a perfect glow on the distant sky—a sunrise as beautiful as the morning deserves. The kind of sunrise that people will take photos of, even though the photos will probably be forgotten and never looked at again. It's strange how people are so desperate to capture their enjoyment that they forget to actually feel it at the time.

The coffee machine beeps. Does that mean it's done? Seems so.

I pour the coffee into the two mugs and carry them upstairs.

When I enter, Olivia is sitting up, scrolling through her phone. The duvet sits beneath her breasts. It's odd that she doesn't want to cover herself up. I'm used to women concealing their bodies as they quickly put on their dress from the previous night, then hurry out of the door before I can make small talk.

Not Olivia. She isn't trying to make me leave, or to cover up what she doesn't want me to see. She is sitting there without a single thought to how exposed she is.

I place the coffee on her bedside table. She thanks me. I get back into bed on the other side and sip my drink.

"I'm not being rude," she says, still scrolling through her phone. "I'm just reading a news article about Billy."

"Oh yeah?"

"Says he's been transferred to a mental health facility where he is being held under strict security."

I scoff. "At least it's better than prison, I guess."

"There are rumours that exorcists came to meet him in prison. The Church has denied all rumours."

I sigh.

I don't need to say anything. It's exactly what I expected.

Olivia shakes her head to herself, puts her phone away, then turns to me and rests her arm across my chest.

"How do you do it?" she asks.

"Do what?"

"Save people's lives, then keep it to yourself. You live in

secrecy when people should celebrate what you did."

"Do you need people to celebrate what we do?"

She considers this. "I guess not. The people who matter already know."

"The people who matter?"

Does she mean me?

I'm not sure I've ever mattered before.

It sounds pathetic. And dramatic. I know. But it feels strange to be wanted. To be desired. To be in a room with a person who actually wants me there.

My phone rings.

I wonder whether to answer it. Whether to ruin the moment. But she's already stepping out of bed, assuming I'll need some privacy. She walks into the bathroom and closes the door behind her.

I look at my phone. It's April. How strange it is to see her name and not rush to pick it up.

I answer.

"Hi," I say.

"Hey, Mo. Seen Billy Tate on the news. Good job."

"Yeah. Nice to see the Church are quick to deny it."

"We do what we have to—but that was a tough case, you did well."

"Thanks."

Usually, her praise would be the highlight of my day. Today, I don't feel like talking to her. And it's not just because I'm finding happiness in another woman.

It's because I'm certain I know what she will ask next.

"Listen, I have a question..." She pauses. "I've felt something. A lot of us have. I was wondering if you felt it too?"

"Felt what?"

"I don't know. Some kind of disturbance. Like a shift in balance. Like Hell is stronger. I'm not sure, it just feels... I don't know, a bit like it did before."

"Before?"

"Yes, like when the balance between Heaven and Hell shifted. Do you know of anything that might have happened? Any reason we need to worry about another war, or anything like that?"

I stare at the bathroom door.

And I consider whether to tell the truth.

Whether to explain what we faced in Billy. What is potentially inside Olivia. How we did battle with the essence of evil.

But what would be the point?

It is done.

Whatever is inside of Olivia cannot thrive without what was inside of Billy.

And if the Church knew, then what would that mean for Olivia?

Would they let her live after what happened last time?

Is it worth the risk?

"No," I say.

"No?"

"No. Nothing at all."

"Oh, okay. I was just wondering, that's all."

"Of course, it's worth checking out."

"Well, I've got to go now—speak to you soon."

"Bye."

She hangs up.

I put the phone down.

A few minutes later, Olivia walks out of the bathroom. She returns to bed. Kisses me.

"Anything important?" she asks.

I consider this, then say, "No."

And she kisses me again.

And I understand what it's like to be happy—truly happy—for what is probably the first time in my life.

And it feels perfect.

Epilogue

Except it's not perfect, is it?

Because Mo cannot see—whether through love, or through tricks of The Devil—what is in front of him.

He seems to have forgotten what is inside of her, and what is growing in strength.

It corrupts his understanding; hides his truth; conceals the memory of what happened.

Because when Olivia sat over Billy, and opened her mouth, and sucked out whatever was inside of him, Mo should not have simply accepted this.

He should have asked—where did it go?

If it was on the ground, would it not have squirmed? Would he not have felt it? Seen its true form when others might not?

If it was in the air, would it not have floated away in a cloud of fire and grey smoke? Would it not have been visible to a sensitive? Would it not have been clear what was happening?

If it disappeared, would he not have felt its presence leave? Felt the difference in his surroundings? Understood that it was gone?

As it was, he didn't ask such questions. Didn't so much as consider them. Didn't even contemplate or ask or suggest or wonder.

Because it didn't wish him to.

Because when it left Billy, it did not go far. Energy can't just disappear. It must leave one vessel and enter another.

If you pour out the dust from an urn, it does not just vanish, does it?

So as Mo sits there, falling in love, doting upon a woman like a love-struck fool, he cannot see what Olivia cannot see either.

She is unaware.

It is how it wants it.

I mean, it was all too easy, wasn't it?

To think that an evil of that grandeur, that they had failed to banish on so many attempts, would just leave; that a mortal man could banish from his body; that a woman's reminder of his family could give him strength to conquer an evil so great; that a renewed vigour might have strengthened his fight... such thoughts are simply preposterous.

Do they not know what they were fighting?

Do they not realise, or deduce, or conceive, of what Billy was harbouring inside of him?

Do they truly believe it was making Billy writhe, making Billy squirm, stopping his breath, all so Olivia could easily defeat it?

Olivia kisses Mo. They make love. They order pizza. They watch television, and they make love again.

They do all the things love-struck fools do.

They take up time. Lots of it. Doing little, but feeling a lot.

It is the time it needs.

To meld.

To entwine.

To grow.

Neither of them see it, hiding behind the twinkle in her eyes.

The days go on, and the weeks go on, and he never leaves her home, and she works and he reads and she laughs and he smiles, and it's all so pathetic—it's all so *human*.

It won't last long.

The humans will fail.

They always do.

When it comes to Hell, they always do.

Be sober-minded.

Be watchful.

Your adversary, The Devil, prowls around like a roaring lion, seeking someone to devour.

For Satan disguises himself as an angel of light.

That is, until the light gives way to darkness.

And you'll wonder why you never saw it.

And you'll wonder when the pain will stop.

And you'll wonder; strive to know; endeavour to discover; how you mortal humans could ever be so stupid.

The only obstacle for The Devil is time—which is something these people have little of.

Book Three is Out in 2024

While you are waiting for Book Three...

Why not read The Edward King Series?

I Have the Sight
Descendant of Hell
An Exorcist Possessed
Blood of Hope
The World Ends Tonight

Join Rick Wood's Reader's Group...

And get three eBooks for free

Join at **www.rickwoodwriter.com/sign-up**

Also by Rick Wood

BLOOD SPLATTER BOOKS

18+

HAUNTED HOUSE

RICK WOOD

www.ingramcontent.com/pod-product-compliance
Lightning Source LLC
LaVergne TN
LVHW041623060526
838200LV00040B/1417